THE CRISIS

A NOVEL

KYLE CORNELL

The Chronal Crisis

The Chronal Crisis

To anyone who has enjoyed The Astrolabe Trilogy – thank you.

"Machines have less problems. I'd like to be a machine, wouldn't you?"

−ANDY WARHOL

CHAPTER ONE

"Well, you've really done it now. How *dare* you! You've made a *complete* mess of the Timeline!" the floating figure scolded.

Cole fell to his knees in shock and shielded his eyes with his hands; he felt like he was suddenly in the presence of a human-shaped star that had somehow been dropped into the middle of his father's laboratory. Dazzling beams of sparkling yellow light consumed the spacious room, spilling over the walls and floor, nearly blinding everyone inside.

"Wh-What are you talking about? WHAT THE HELL ARE YOU?!" Brody yelled in disbelief. He was shaking and hiding underneath a table.

"Well, that's a very rude thing to ask someone!" the glowing figure grumbled. "But if you must know, I am...um...actually, it will take too long to explain. Right now, all you need to know is that you must come with me. Please?" Their voice was commanding and had a slight echo to it, like an uptight and bossy schoolmarm who just so happened to be speaking directly into a portable fan.

"Are you kidding?" Arthur asked in disbelief. He squinted his eyes in order to look at the floating figure. "You can't just appear out of nowhere and start ordering us around!"

The glowing being turned their head and frowned. Or, rather, Cole assumed that they frowned – it was difficult to determine, since their facial features were a glowing blur. With a sound like fluttering wings, they floated over to Arthur and levitated directly in front of him.

"I *can* and I *will,* Arthur Bennett. Now, please remain silent and follow directions -- for once. Enough damage has been caused because of your stubbornness and impulsivity."

"Damage? What do you mean?" he asked, a slight edge to his voice.

"I'll give you all to the count of three. Move yourselves next to me. 1...2..."

But before the glowing figure could finish counting, Brody screamed, "RUNNNN!" and, as if on cue, Cole, Gabe, Brody, Karma, and Ruby turned and bolted out of the laboratory.

"Hey! Come back!" the glowing figure yelled.

Karma and Ruby raced up the entrance lobby staircase to look for somewhere to hide, while Cole, without thinking about where he was going, streaked down the hallway, Gabe right behind him, and ran into the nearest closet – a storage room full of cleaning supplies. They slammed the door, slid the lock shut, and backed slowly into the dark room.

"What is that -- that *thing?!*" Gabe whispered. His breath came in sharp gasps.

"I have no idea! Is Project Hominum attacking us again?"

"Oh dear, not those crazy bigots," said a voice behind them.

When the boys turned around, they jumped in surprise -- the luminous intruder was there, floating in midair! Their arms were crossed across their gleaming chest.

"*What do you want?!*" Cole screamed.

"I already told you -- you and your friends must come with me. There is a crisis that you need to fix!"

"GET AWAY FROM US!"

Cole picked up a dusty mop bucket and chucked it at the intruder; it passed through the floating being's head and hit the opposite wall. Cole and Gabe ran out of the room, and, with a sigh of frustration, the glowing figure floated after them.

Things continued like this for the next several minutes. Cole and Gabe ran from room to room, looking for anywhere to hide, but it was no use -- no matter where they went, the gleaming figure was there.

"STOP RUNNING AWAY FROM ME!" they bellowed, always one step behind the panicked pair.

Finally, after deciding to give up and flee the manor house, the boys clattered down the entrance lobby staircase with thundering footsteps. Gabe threw open the front doors and they stumbled outside.

However, before they even made it out of the front gate, they skidded to a halt so as not to run into Brody, Ruby, and Karma. All three of them were standing in a horizontal line, staring out at something.

"There you are!" Cole said. "Come on, we have to...to keep run..."

The chaos that stretched out in front of him took his breath away, nearly bowling him over. A jagged, angry crack raced down the street, buckling the pavement and tearing open a deep chasm that swallowed trees, parked cars, and even several skyscrapers. The monstrous crevice stretched on and on for thirty city blocks. A thick layer of smoke hovered above the city.

What Cole couldn't see, further down the block, was much, much worse: damaged fire hydrants spewed fountains of water into the air; a deafening mixture of car alarms and pained screams provided the soundtrack for the surrounding pandemonium; dozens of firetrucks had been deployed to help stranded citizens escape from their crumbling apartment buildings. Just above the misery and destruction, a red sky churned and swirled like an ocean that was caught up in a hurricane. Cole's mouth hung open in horror as he looked around at these grim surroundings.

"What happened here?" Gabe whispered. "Mechanica City looks even worse now!"

"But, we...we fixed it! Right? We fixed time!" Brody cried out in disbelief.

"You most certainly did not. There are *many* other issues that still need to be addressed," said a stern voice behind them. Cole jumped in surprise and turned around – right on schedule, the glowing being was floating next to him. Everyone screamed.

"Alright, that's *quite* enough. No offense, but all of you are so dramatic. After everything you've seen on *The Astrolabe,* you're shocked by someone like *me?*"

"Go away!" Ruby yelled. She winced and shielded her eyes from the light.

"Oh my goodness...am I too bright?"

"YES!" everyone screamed in unison.

"My apologies! One moment, please." The human-shaped star rose into the air and, with a spin, lowered the intensity of their glow, as if they had their own internal dimming switch.

"There. Is that better?"

"Much," Gabe answered.

"What…What is your name?" Karma whispered. Her legs were shaking with fear. "Are you some kind of an angel?"

"My name is Thelonia. No, I'm not an angel, but I promise you that all of your questions will be answered soon. I'm on a very strict schedule, you see. Right now, my only duty is to escort you to Atmos where my superior will give you your instructions."

"Atmos? What is that?" Brody asked.

"Hold on, you keep mentioning a crisis. What exactly did we do?" Cole asked.

Thelonia scoffed and looked at him incredulously. "You can't be serious! Have you already forgotten about the MASSIVE wormhole that you left *wide open* in the Mesozoic Era?"

"How do you know about that?" Cole asked nervously. Where did this being get its information from?

"Let's just say that my superior is well-informed," Thelonia answered. "Much more than you could possibly imagine. In fact, he and I have direct knowledge concerning the Master Timeline."

"The what?" Ruby asked quizzically. All of these new terms were making her head spin.

"Now. Take a look around you. What do you see?"

"Ummm chaos? Destruction?" Gabe offered.

"Exactly. Everything is an *utter ruin,* a complete disaster now!" Thelonia cried. Her voice started getting louder and more irritated. "A disaster that you and your friends DIRECTLY CAUSED!"

An awkward silence fell. With a deep, steadying breath, the irritable being paused and took a moment to calm down.

The front doors of the manor house were suddenly thrown open and Arthur and Sabina came stumbling out, Arthur leaning on his crutches.

"GET AWAY FROM THEM!" Sabina bellowed.

Arthur thrust his blaster into the air and fired off a warning shot. A crackling sound reverberated in everyone's ears.

"What are you going to do? Shoot me?" Thelonia asked, their voice dripping with sarcasm. "As you can see, I'm not exactly solid."

"Put the gun down, Dad!" Ruby scolded. "This...um...*being*...was just talking about that wormhole that you created. Remember? The one in the Mesozoic Era?"

Arthur's face paled. "H-How do you know about that?"

"I've seen it! *Time itself has almost been destroyed!*" Thelonia bellowed.

The glowing being's harsh and accusatory words cast a strained silence over Cole and the group. Everyone looked at each other, shock and confusion etched onto their faces. Could Thelonia actually be telling the truth?

"No...No, that's impossible. I don't mean to sound pretentious, but I'm fairly certain that I know more about time travel, quantum physics, and wormholes than most people, yet even I was unable to find a way to close the tear. But I promise you, according to my research, it's completely harmless if you just leave it alone," Arthur explained.

"*HARMLESS?!* It certainly isn't harmless! I'm sorry, sir, but that attitude just confirms what I've always thought about you: you're unspeakably arrogant."

"Now, wait a minute!" Cole cried.

"Only one as arrogant as you would experiment with time when *they have no idea what they're doing!*"

Arthur's face burned with frustration. "Listen…it wasn't my intention to cause any problems, OK? I'm obviously willing to discuss ways that I can fix things. So, stop bothering my family and just take this up with me."

Thelonia bobbed in the air and smiled. "Well…I appreciate you saying that. I really do. But actions have consequences, so you still need to speak with my superior. All of you. Now, will you come quietly? Or will I have to use force?"

Force? The word stuck uncomfortably inside Cole's ear like a bur. He locked eyes with Arthur and Sabina; they shook their heads slightly and their hands folded over their blasters. The message was clear -- no one was going anywhere with this strange being, no matter what demands they made. What if Thelonia took them somewhere dangerous? Or led them into a trap? They needed more time to think and to assess all the available information – which wasn't much.

Karma took a step forward and approached Thelonia. "Excuse me, but I have to step in here. My friends and I aren't going anywhere with you. Why should we trust you? This situation is completely ridiculous."

Thelonia closed their eyes and let out a beleaguered sigh. "Very well. Don't say that I didn't ask nicely."

With a swiping motion of their hand, pairs of handcuffs that were constructed out of shimmering white light suddenly wrapped themselves around Arthur and Sabina's wrists.

"What is this? Take these off!" Arthur said.

"Guards!" Thelonia cried.

With a loud rushing sound, two additional glowing figures suddenly appeared. They were a similar shape and height as Thelonia. The two figures slowly floated down next to Arthur and Sabina, who struggled desperately to run away, but, strangely, their feet were now stuck to the ground.

"Let them go!" Ruby yelled. "Who gave you the authority to do this?"

"You'll have a chance to speak with him very soon," Thelonia replied. With another swiping hand gesture, the glowing being brought forth a shining bubble that was constructed out of radiant yellow light. It hovered in the air and grew bigger and bigger, swelling like a helium balloon. Like cloying hands, the bubble stretched and folded itself around Cole and the rest of the group, locking them inside. Cole, his eyes bulging in panic, pounded desperately on the walls of the bubble, but it was no use – they were trapped.

The air directly in front of everyone began to change. Large ripples spread out, swirling and wobbling, bending the physical space around them. A roaring noise filled everyone's ears, and, with a flash, a bright white light enveloped them and they disappeared.

CHAPTER TWO

When the roaring sound in Cole's ears finally subsided, he found himself lying face down on a warm, glossy floor. With a groan, he slowly sat up, massaged his throbbing head, and opened his eyes. The brightest light that he had ever seen was shining all around him, as if he was sitting in the very center of the Sun. He winced and slammed his eyes shut again.

"*Agh!* Hello? Thelonia? Is anyone there? I-I can't see!"

"Oh, right. Sorry! I keep forgetting that you aren't of this world. Here, these will help." Thelonia spread their fingers wide, clapped their hands together, and then pulled them apart. In between their hands, several pairs of glasses with dark lenses came into being out of thin air. The glowing figure tossed a pair to everyone.

As soon as Cole pulled the glasses down over his eyes, he stared at Thelonia in wonder – their glowing captor now appeared as a tall and beautiful woman with long, golden hair. Her nose was slender, and her plump lips were a deep crimson color. She was draped in voluminous maroon robes that fell to the floor.

The bright light faded and everything came into sharp focus. Cole gasped -- he and his friends were now standing in the middle of an empty hall that appeared to be the length of a football field. It stretched on and on in front of them before abruptly taking a sharp turn to the left.

Above them soared a domed roof. It appeared to have been carved out of thousands of slabs of gold, and, hanging from it, placed in equal intervals, was a long row of heavy crystal chandeliers that held dozens of white candles. The walls that enclosed the hall were covered with thick marble panels.

His mind buzzing, Cole slowly turned his head to the right and his eyes fell upon a row of identical French doors with gold frames that looked out onto a large, carefully tended hedge garden that was standing in the middle of vast estate grounds. Bright green hedges had been arranged in whimsical, curated formations. He also spotted other glowing beings like Thelonia, but, with his glasses on, they appeared as robed humans floating around the grounds.

"Where are we?" Gabe asked.

"Welcome to Atmos," Thelonia answered. "We call this a bubble universe. The glasses are giving your surroundings mass and weight so that you're able to see them. An interesting bit of temporal technology."

"A bubble *what?!*"

"Oh, and guards? Take those two away," Thelonia ordered.

The two guards, who now appeared as human men clad in polished armor, roughly grabbed Arthur and Sabina by the arms. Cole's father and his girlfriend, along with the guards, abruptly vanished like a flame being extinguished.

"Where did they take them?" Cole yelled. "Don't hurt them!"

"We'll be keeping them in a cell for now, just until my boss decides what to do with them," Thelonia explained. "Don't worry, they'll be well protected."

"*A cell?!*" Ruby cried in shock.

"Well...I'm sorry, but Arthur only has himself to blame for that. But, if it makes you feel any better, they won't be alone. Other guests will be joining them."

"What does that mean?" Gabe asked suspiciously.

"I have a few errands to run, so I must be going. Please take a look around and enjoy the sights. I will find you in an hour or so." Thelonia gave a small wave and floated away.

Brody, Gabe, Ruby, Karma, and Cole looked at each other in disbelief and were silent for several minutes. What was there to say? They were stranded in an unknown world with absolutely no sense of direction and no way to get back home.

"So...what should we do now?" Brody finally asked.

"This is *insane,*" Gabe said. "HELLOOOO?" His voice echoed throughout the empty hall.

"Well...we don't have many options. Thelonia told us to take a look around, so maybe we should just do that. See if we can get a better sense of our surroundings while we wait for her to come back," Karma suggested.

Since no one else had a better idea, they all nodded in agreement and made their way down the long hall.

For the next hour and a half, the group tentatively explored this new world that they'd been unceremoniously dropped into. Walking down the hall, they passed by gold sculptured guéridons and tall mirrors with Baroque frames. Thick beams of soft light poured in through the French doors and dappled the floor. Everything was quiet and still.

They turned a corner and came upon another empty hall, but this time the marble walls were covered with a random collection of doors. They were all different shapes, sizes, and textures; some were jewel toned and so large that a dump truck could easily pass through, whereas others were the size of a postcard and made from brass. Behind each of the doors was a room that held something unique and unexpected: a glittering plaza square that was dominated by a gushing stone fountain; a floor-to-ceiling mirrored dance hall that was silent and empty of all music; an enormous restaurant with a decorative ceiling.

Despite their exciting interiors, however, each room felt dusty and lifeless. Unease filled Cole's stomach. He couldn't explain it, but a sense of abandonment and buried feelings seemed to hover over everything. He shivered and kept walking.

Eventually they turned another corner that led to yet another hall and collection of doors. The largest door, solid gold with swirling, decorative trim and a glittering doorknob, stood by itself.

"Ooh, look at this!" Brody said, his eyes wide with wonder. He moved to the door and grabbed the doorknob. Unfortunately, no matter how hard he pulled, it remained firmly shut.

After exploring a few more halls in the mysterious mansion (or was it a castle?), Cole and his group of friends decided to switch things up and see what was on the other side of the line of French doors. They walked down a short flight of stone steps and onto soft green grass. A warm breeze blew by them. The sloping lawns of the estate grounds were eerily quiet; not even the sound of chirping birds could be heard.

They strolled through the hedge garden, green boxwood plants and privets standing in long rows on either side of them. Everyone was quiet as they walked, assessing their myriad of new problems. This group had been through a lot together, but they had never encountered a dilemma this substantial before; they all struggled to keep their anxiety in check.

"How are we going to get out of this?" Cole asked Ruby.

"Honestly? I don't even know where to start. I'm completely out of ideas," she replied morosely.

"Well, at least that Thelonia ghost-person seems nice enough," Gabe said.

"She does?" Karma quipped.

"We just have to be smart about this. If we stay calm and do whatever her boss says, they'll have to send us back home."

Through a large arched hedge, they suddenly stumbled upon a figure that was floating in the air. Their glasses made this being appear to them as a woman with lanky grey hair that fell to her shoulders. She bobbed up and down in the air, draped in heavy robes, and stared at the ground.

"Hello!" Brody said cheerfully.

The woman screamed and turned in their direction. Her large eyes darted from left to right and she began to wring her hands nervously.

"Ma'am? Is everything OK?" Ruby asked.

The woman opened her mouth and attempted to speak, but the words died on her lips. No sound would come out.

Why won't she say anything? Cole wondered.

Tears welled up in her eyes and she let out a heavy sigh. Then, looking around as if she was desperately checking for something, she turned and floated away like a frightened rabbit.

"What was that all about?" Karma asked.

"No idea," Gabe said. "Can we get out of here? This garden is starting to creep me out."

Ten minutes later, as the group made their way down the halls, Thelonia suddenly materialized in front of them.

"There you are! It's time. My boss is ready to see you now," she said.

"When are you going to release my father and his girlfriend?" Cole asked.

Thelonia smiled a tight smile. "I feel like I've said this *a thousand times,* but I'll say it once more – Aloicius will answer all your questions, OK? Now, follow me please. We mustn't keep him waiting."

CHAPTER THREE

The group followed Thelonia, her long, golden hair billowing behind her as she floated along, leading them down one of the long halls. After two lefts and a right, they finally came to a stop in front of a wide and glittering silver door. Armored guards stood silently on either side of it.

"What is this place?" Gabe asked, looking up at the massive door in awe.

"This is Saxum Hall, where our most important meetings are conducted. This is also where Aloicius resides."

Like a lens diaphragm, a hole suddenly opened in the center of the silver door, and after everyone had stepped through it, the opening closed behind them. Cole gulped nervously.

As they entered Saxum Hall, the craggy walls of a massive stone cavern rose up around them. The cavern was circular in shape, and its walls dripped with water. Cole's eyes passed over four colossal glass columns that held up a ceiling that was dotted with sharp stalactites.

Men and women wearing long robes hovered in large groups throughout the room, their eyes locked onto a flat black disc that had been placed in the center of the room. It looked to Cole like it was constructed out of leather or some kind of unique rubber.

Thelonia lowered her voice down to a stern whisper. "Aloicius will arrive shortly. *Do not* speak disrespectfully to him. He is a man of immense importance."

Brody rolled his eyes. Thelonia glared at him and then floated out of the room.

Moments later, a small cloud of shimmering gold smoke started swirling above the black disc. The robed men and women in the room exchanged nervous looks. Then, the smoke molded itself into a massive hologram of a man's head. Through his glasses, Cole could see a middle-aged face that was deeply weathered and humorless. Bushy grey eyebrows rested beneath a prominent forehead, and sagging cheeks were streaked with deep lines. Aloicius's hooded eyes had icy blue irises, and his steely gaze seemed to pierce through everyone in the room.

The hologram face slowly blinked and turned to look at the group of friends. Cole gulped and shook with nervousness.

"Welcome, Cole Bennett. Welcome, Cole Bennett's family and friends. My name is Aloicius. I've invited you here today for a very important task."

"'Invited' isn't exactly the word that I would use," Brody grumbled.

Aloicius's eyes flashed dangerously but he didn't respond to the comment.

"Anyway...I have invited you to this bubble universe because --"

"I'm still so confused. What *is* a bubble universe?" Gabe asked.

"A bubble universe is a small, self-contained universe. This one exists just outside of the Master Timeline. They can be designed to be as expansive as you would like, but this one is very small; the boundaries only extend to the edge of the estate grounds."

"Why does it look like Versailles here?" Brody asked.

"Well, I was given the opportunity to choose what this universe looks like, and I've always held a fascination with the palace of Versailles, so..."

"You created this, um, bubble universe?" Cole asked.

"No. The ones who created me brought this place into existence. They simply allowed me to design it. No, I'm just the caretaker. My solemn duty is to watch over the Master Timeline and ensure that it always flows the way that it is meant to. When it becomes diseased and unstable, like it is now, all of reality hangs in the balance."

"Who created you?"

"My masters call themselves The Elders. Little is known of their origin, for they have always existed and they tend to keep their secrets hidden from anyone but themselves. What I can tell you, though, is that they are immensely wise and powerful. They created the Master Timeline. Or, said another way, all of space and time."

A tense and heavy silence filled the chamber. Cole started feeling lightheaded. His chest burned with anxiety, and it was becoming difficult to breathe. He could see the same look of dread reflected in his friend's and family's eyes. No one knew what to say. Elders? Master Timeline? All of it was overwhelming and confusing.

"This is...a lot to take in," Cole admitted. "And I-I'm sorry, but I still don't know why we're here. Thelonia didn't really tell us anything." His stomach was tangled in anxious knots, and speaking to this massive, imposing head wasn't helping his nerves, but he desperately wanted answers.

"I could explain it to you, but it will be easier if I show you," Aloicius answered. His holographic face abruptly dissolved and was replaced by an image that Cole never thought he would see again. They were now looking at a wide, low valley that was dotted with small shrubs. Peculiar trees with multicolored branches swayed in the background. At the bottom of the valley, a colossal wormhole bobbed up and down in the air. Orange crystals jutted out of the ground beneath it, and they were being yanked and pulled, almost ripping out of the soil due to the force of the wind.

"The Mesozoic Era," Ruby whispered.

Strong gusts of wind and crackling electricity poured out of the wormhole. The edges of the portal vibrated and twisted with a snarling energy.

"Do you remember this?" said the voice of Aloicius. "The wormhole that your father opened? And then he didn't do anything to seal it?"

"Well...he didn't just leave it there on purpose," Cole said sheepishly. "He just...you know...didn't know how to close it."

"Then why was he experimenting with time travel? When he didn't know *every single facet* of it?"

"Well --"

"That's extremely dangerous!" Aloicius's voice bellowed. The image of the wormhole disappeared and his face returned.

Cole winced and his stomach sank miserably. He let out a frustrated sigh before answering.

"It-It's a long story, so you'd have to ask my father those questions. B-But I promise you that he is a very intelligent and sensible man! This whole situation has truly been an honest mistake." His nerves were becoming increasingly frayed, and his knees began to shake. Aloicius was extremely intimidating. Cole just wanted this conversation to end.

"Well...that may be true, but the fact remains that the wormhole must be sealed. Now, when you went back in time and solved that situation with Oscar Wilde, the resulting chronal shockwaves that were generated have caused the Time Tear to open even wider. As you saw, it's enormous. It won't be stable for much longer. And, if that wasn't bad enough, now it's acting like a black hole -- anything that gets near it is sucked inside. The Master Timeline is close to collapsing; specific points in time have been scrambled and changed, ones that we call 'linchpin events,' and they have had far-reaching effects on many other events throughout history. You must seal the Time Tear."

"But, how do we do that?" Karma asked.

"Well, luckily for all of you, I have a tool that will help. I call it the Gödel Brush. All you have to do is point the bristles at the edges of the portal and push a button. The wormhole will be permanently sealed shut."

Aloicius opened his mouth and a square paintbrush shot out, slid across the floor, and stopped at Cole's feet. The paintbrush had a wooden handle and glittering bristles. It was bigger than Cole's hand.

"So...not to be rude or anything, but if you had this tool this whole time, not to mention that you and the people in this room are all-powerful spirits, why couldn't you fix this issue?" Brody asked.

The crowds of people standing in the room flashed shocked expressions in his direction.

Aloicius frowned and paused for a moment. A nervous sweat rolled down Cole's back. Was he going to punish them now?

"My people, the Uhrzeit, are the men and women that you see standing in this room. They were created to help me monitor the Master Timeline and report any discrepancies that occur. However, they, along with myself, consist of a combination of light and temporal energy – no one here is 'all-powerful.' While we can navigate the Master Timeline, we can't manipulate physical objects. But you all are human. You are constructed out of organic matter and mass, so you will be able to manipulate the Gödel Brush."

"But...what about those Time Beast things? They can eat stray wormholes and stuff. Can't they fix this?" Gabe asked.

"Time Beasts? What are you talking about?"

"You know, those translucent creatures that swim alongside *The Astrolabe*."

"Ah, you must be referring to the *tempesti*. They have existed since the very beginning of time itself, when the Master Timeline was newly formed. But alas, due to the severe damage to the Timeline, all the *tempesti* have died."

"All of them?" Karma asked in alarm.

"Yes, all of them. The temperature inside the space between the decades has become unstable. It fluctuates wildly now, and the *tempesti* can't survive under the current conditions."

Cole's stomach rolled with nausea at the thought of hundreds of bloated *tempesti* corpses floating around.

"Well, I guess that means we won't have to worry about any of them going rogue and possessing people again," Brody quipped.

"What do we need to do to fix the Timeline?" Gabe asked.

The hologram face morphed once again, and, this time, a long and horizontal chart appeared in its place. On the chart was a straight line with hundreds of dates branching off, above and beneath it. Five red dots glowed over specific dates on the chart.

"What you are looking at is a map of the Master Timeline. The glowing dots represent the moments in time that you will need to travel to," Aloicius's voice explained. "You'll be going to Pasadena, California in 1953, then move on to 1927 Paris, followed by Washington, D.C. in 1835, Boston in 1773, and then, finally, the Mesozoic Era. The past must unfold in the manner that it's meant to unfold."

"Why can't we just go straight to the Mesozoic Era and close the wormhole?" Brody asked. "Won't that reset everything?"

"Oh no," Aloicius said firmly. "It doesn't work like that. The damage caused to the Master

Timeline must be repaired first, and then you can focus on sealing the wormhole."

"Won't we make the Time Tear larger if we go and fix these linchpin events?" Cole asked.

"No. Using a bit of complicated temporal engineering, I have put in place a temporary freeze onto the Timeline. There will be no negative consequences. However, it won't hold forever, so you must hurry."

"But...what happens if we fail?" Karma asked.

Aloicius's expression darkened. "It will be devastating. The Master Timeline will fold in on itself and all of reality will end."

Another strained silence fell over the group. The stakes couldn't be higher.

"But, before that happens, you have a chance to set things right. Now, your journey will be perilous -- "

"Stop. I need to speak," Ruby said.

Aloicius frowned. "*Yes?*"

"You're acting like I'm just going to agree to this. Wh...What if I don't?" she asked, a slight tremble to her voice. "I mean, I had nothing to do with creating that wormhole. And besides, I-I'm not well. Not myself yet. I've just gone through an *extremely* traumatic experience and I...I just...*no*. You can't ask me to do this."

"Ruby!" Cole cried.

Aloicius narrowed his eyes. "You will do as I say. I know that you have been through a dramatic ordeal. I've seen it. But my entire purpose as the caretaker of the Timeline, for millennia, has been to monitor it and ensure that events unfold in the way that they are meant to unfold. That is the *only* thing that matters to me, not the petty problems of human

33

beings. So, if you ever expect to see your world again, not to mention your father and his girlfriend, then you will complete this task."

Red spots bloomed on Ruby's cheeks, and she twisted her mouth angrily.

"*Excuse me?* I'm not going to allow a *giant head* to threaten me or give me orders, do you understand me? *No one* tells me what to do. I'm not doing this mission!" she roared. Her eyes blazed with fire.

"Ruby, *stop!* Why are you doing this?!" Cole shouted.

"Shut up, Cole! You have no idea what I've been through!"

"Come on, Ruby, don't be like this," Gabe chastised.

"*NO!* I'm not going to let you talk me out of this!"

She started pacing wildly back and forth, a frantic plan forming quickly in her mind. "I'm...I'm going to track down Gustav Fallowback. Yes, that's what I'll do! And I'll make him pay for what was done to me. I mean, if I'm not able to confront my actual abuser, I'll confront the man who put him up to it. And there's not a *damn* thing anyone can do to stop me!"

She breathed heavily, balled her fists, and glared at Aloicius, practically begging him to contradict her. Cole had never seen her look so furious.

"Ruby, you sound crazy. Where did this idea even come from? You should let the mayor handle Project Hominum. And what about Dad and Sabina? You're just going to abandon them?" Cole asked roughly.

Ruby turned and looked at him with such an intense expression of pain that it scared him. Tears were pouring down her face.

"*Please,* Cole. I'm not strong enough. I can't go on a journey like this, I...I won't survive it..." She brought her hands to her face and began to sob in earnest.

"Your, um, Eminence?" Karma asked. Everyone in the room stared at her. With a determined expression on her face, she slowly walked over to Ruby and put her arms around her. "It's OK, darling. Aloicius, sir, please. I also have my own score to settle with Mr. Fallowback, as I'm sure you know. I would like to accompany Ruby."

Ruby smiled and wiped the tears from her eyes. "Thank you. I would *love it* if you came with me. I could really use your help."

Aloicius closed his heavily lidded eyes and silently pondered their request. Several tense minutes passed by.

"Hmm...I will accept this," he slowly mumbled, finally speaking. "This mission won't require all of you, and, as you said, neither of you were directly involved with opening the wormhole. You may return to your own time, but you will have to leave right now."

"Ruby? Karma? Are you *seriously* going to leave right now? How will you stay safe?" Cole asked, his voice cracking with emotion.

"We'll be fine, Cole. We'll have each other. Please try to understand -- we have to do this," Karma said.

"Well...at least take this." Cole moved to her and handed her a portable radio. "If you ever get in trouble or want to find us, use this radio. We need to stay in touch."

Aloicius watched as Cole and Karma hugged tightly.

"Guards?" he barked.

Ruby and Karma turned and looked at Cole, Brody, and Gabe with conflicted expressions on their faces as they were escorted out of the room by two guards.

"Wait a minute!" Brody suddenly yelled.

Oh God, what now? Cole thought miserably. The lightheaded feeling in his head was getting stronger, and spots started popping in front of his eyes. Their group, their small family, was falling apart, and there was nothing he could do to stop it.

"I can't do this either! Time travel is way too much for me. There's...There's too much responsibility. *Please.* I'm mentally exhausted," Brody admitted. "I can help Mechanica City rebuild while Cole and Gabe save the Timeline!"

"Absolutely not. No one else is leaving. It will take more than two people to complete this extremely important mission. You will need all the help that you can get. I've already been more than generous --"

"*What?!* That's not fair! You just let them go --"

"ENOUGH!" Aloicius roared. Dust fell from the cavern roof. "My word is final. You must prepare to leave. *Now.*"

Brody's face clouded with anger. "Or what?"

Aloicius let out a low chuckle. "I like your gumption, young man. But it won't help you here. If you choose not to participate in the mission, I'll simply stick you with Arthur and Sabina. Hopefully you will complete this mission quickly. The clock is ticking."

Brody's mouth fell open in shock. No words came out. He slowly moved back to stand next to Cole and Gabe and shook with rage.

"Now, as I said before, you are organic beings. You won't be able to teleport through the Master Timeline like we can, so, that infernal train called *The Astrolabe* must be utilized to complete this mission. Here is some information about each altered moment in time that you will be fixing," Aloicius said. He opened his mouth again and another item popped out. This time, it was a small scroll of paper. Gabe picked it up off the floor.

"Now -- get to it," Aloicius said pointedly.

Waves of panic rolled through Cole's body, and he tried to take deep breaths as sweat poured down his face.

"Can...Can we please talk to my father before we leave?"

Aloicius sighed deeply. "Do you have to?"

"*Please.*"

"All of you are so demanding...but fine. You may speak with him. I'll give you ten minutes, and then you *must* leave. There is no time to waste." The hologram faded and Aloicius's face disappeared.

"Cole? Are you OK?" Gabe asked. He was staring at his jittery boyfriend with deep concern on his face.

Cole swayed where he stood. His vision began to fade as his panic attack reached its zenith.

"I...I don't feel good..."

Then, he stumbled over his feet and sank to the ground.

CHAPTER FOUR

Cole was awakened by a palm slapping him across the face.

"H-Hey!"

Gabe looked down at him with a worried expression. "There you are! Are you OK? Come on, let's get you up." He grabbed Cole's hand and helped him to his feet.

At first, Cole thought that he was standing inside a shadowy wine cellar, but as his eyes adjusted to the light from the wall torches, he realized that he was actually in a short hallway. On each side of the hallway were rows of damp and cold jail cells. The cells had been carved into the stone walls, and each one was small and enclosed with thick metal bars.

"How are you feeling?"

"I'll survive. Wh-What happened?"

"I...I think you had a panic attack," Gabe answered quietly. A strained and concerned expression rested on his face.

Cole groaned in frustration and a nauseating wave of shame rolled through him. "I'm sorry. This is *so* embarrassing. I'm...I'm really trying to get my anxiety under control."

"No need to apologize, son. We understand," a voice said.

Cole turned and saw Arthur and Sabina standing in one of the jail cells. A pair of strangers, a man and woman with dark black hair, were inside with them. He walked over to their jail cell and grabbed the bars.

"How are you doing? Are you hurt?"

"We're doing great," Arthur replied, trying to appear cheerful, yet he looked exhausted and leaned heavily on his crutches. "The guards have kept their word and haven't hurt us. Thelonia promised that we'll be fed and my leg will be healed, so it's not too bad."

"Don't act like we're in some kind of luxury hotel, though," the man with the dark hair said irritably. He was leaning against the wall with his arms crossed.

Gabe winced with embarrassment. "Cole, this is my father. My mother, Lucia, is next to him."

Cole suddenly recognized the two strangers in the cell. "Oh, of *course!* It's great to finally meet you, Mr. and Mrs. Hernandez."

"Oh no, it's actually Ramos. Miss Lucia Ramos," Lucia said. "It's nice to meet you, too, although I wish it was under better circumstances."

Cole noticed that Gabe had the same eyes as her.

"I'm Javier. Gabriel has told us a lot about you," Mr. Hernandez said. He shook Cole's hand through the bars of the cell.

"I'm so sorry that you've been dragged into this mess," Cole said.

"Are you here to break us out?" Lucia asked.

"No. At least, not yet anyway. Let me explain."

For the next several minutes, Cole recounted everything that they had learned in the past hour. He described their current surroundings and told them about the new mission that Aloicius had given to them. As he talked, Arthur's face grew more and more pale.

"So, basically, if we don't succeed in this mission, all of reality will end," Cole explained.

"No pressure," Lucia quipped.

"I don't understand why Aloicius or The Elders, who have so much power, can't just use their abilities to fix everything," Arthur said. "It seems strange."

"I don't really get it, either, but that's what Aloicius said," Cole answered.

Javier balled his fists angrily. "So...you're telling me that I might be stuck in this cell for the rest of my life?"

"No, that's not --"

"And I'm stuck here because of something I didn't even do?!"

"Well...it's a bit more complicated than that," Sabina mumbled.

"It's not! This jerk right here is the reason why we're trapped! Come here, you little --" Javier grabbed Arthur by the front of his shirt and pulled his other arm back, ready to punch him in the face.

"Knock it off!" Lucia screamed, and she shoved her hands angrily against Javier's chest, pushing him back.

"No, Javier has every right to be mad!" Brody argued. "We wouldn't even be in this situation if it wasn't for Arthur."

"What the hell, Brody?" Gabe cried.

"And now I'm being forced to go time traveling *yet again!* Things couldn't get any worse!"

Cole turned and glared at him, but Brody turned away.

Arthur looked miserable. He leaned against the wall to steady himself. "I...I didn't want any of this to happen!" he lamented. "All I wanted to do was find my dead wife, and then...things spiraled out of control. But Aloicius and Brody are right. This is my fault. I never should have experimented with time travel, no matter what the reason was. It was dangerous and foolish...I'm so sorry. If I could do this mission myself, I would."

Sabina walked over to him and linked her hand with his. "What's done is done, Arthur."

"She's right," Gabe said. "There's nothing to do now but move forward. We're going to get you all out of there. We'll do whatever Aloicius needs us to do and then everything will go back to normal."

"You actually believe that?" Brody grumbled.

Cole glared at him again. "Are you done?"

"No, I've just gotten started!" Brody yelled back.

"Shut the h-- !"

"STOP IT!" Gabe barked, and the two boys fell silent.

"Wait a minute...where are Ruby and Karma?" Sabina asked.

Cole's spirits sank. "They, um, decided to go back to Mechanica City."

"They did *what?*" Arthur cried.

"Oh dear. Will they be safe? The city is extremely dangerous now," Sabina said.

"We couldn't convince them to stay. They're going to track down that Gustav Fallowback guy."

Arthur massaged the bridge of his nose anxiously, deep in thought.

"Hmm...Gustav is a very old man, so he won't be a physical threat to them. All Ruby has to do is stick with Karma and she'll have a fighting chance. However, I'm sure he still has many powerful connections in the city who can make things difficult for them. I'm also concerned about what they'll do to Gustav when they find him..."

"Do you think Ruby will...you know..." Gabe made a cutting motion across his throat.

Arthur's face looked grim. He didn't answer.

Suddenly, two guards appeared in the hallway. Stern expressions rested on their faces.

"Time to go," one of the guards ordered.

"One last thing!" Arthur said. He grabbed Cole's hand. "Here. I want you to take this spare pocket watch with you. This could help you if you get into any trouble. You can do this. I believe in you."

Cole's bottom lip trembled, and he struggled to appear brave in front of his friends and family. He had never dealt with a more complicated mission, and so much unknown lay ahead of them.

His voice shook as he said, "We'll...We'll be back soon. I promise. We won't let you down."

The guards escorted Cole, Gabe, and Brody away.

CHAPTER FIVE

"I can't *believe* we have to get back on this train again," Brody complained. He was standing next to Cole and Gabe on a Decade Station platform, waiting for *The Astrolabe* to arrive.

Cole prickled with irritation. Within the last hour, his attitude towards Brody had completely soured. His constant whining was making it difficult to focus, and Cole struggled to contain his anger.

"Listen, Brody. This is an incredibly important mission, the most important one that we've ever had. I'm really sorry that you're involved, but you're here now. I don't know what you want us to say."

"Why are you being such a --?"

"Hey, we'll be done in no time," Gabe assured Brody, steering the conversation in a different direction. "We'll stop by a few places, fix a couple of things, and then return to Mechanica City before you even know it!"

Brody frowned in response but didn't say anything more.

At the sound of a sharp whistle, an immense bone-white train appeared from off in the distance and headed towards them, its bulky wheels speeding along fiery train tracks. Just before it approached the Decade Station, the brakes were activated, and the locomotive slowed to a stop in front of the boys. A door on the side of the train opened on its own and they stepped inside.

"Hello! Welcome to – oh! It's lovely to see you all again!" said a young woman wearing a bottle green dress with large puff sleeves. Mrs. Halifax, a mechanical that was constructed out of pieces of iron, was one of a group of four mechanicals that worked as the conductors of *The Astrolabe.*

Brody didn't say anything. He brushed past everyone, went into the nearest train compartment, and slammed the door closed.

"Oh dear. Is everything alright?" Mrs. Halifax asked.

"Yeah...it's a long story. But it's good to see you again. Can we meet in the front?" Gabe asked.

"Certainly!" Mrs. Halifax said, and they followed her down a long, carpeted hallway, through dozens of train cars, before finally arriving in the front compartment.

"So! Where can I take you today?" she asked.

"Well...a few places, but we'll start with 1953," Cole answered. "If we go Express, how long do you think that will take?"

"Hmm...let me check," Mrs. Halifax said. She moved to a control panel, pushed several buttons, and then a string of numbers appeared on a screen. "It will take exactly three hours to reach the 1950's Decade Station."

"Three hours? Hmm," Cole said dejectedly. "Oh well. I wish we could get there faster, but it is what it is. Well...what should we do until we get there?"

"We still need to put together a concrete plan for this mission. Other than that tiny scroll, Aloicius didn't construct one for us before sending us on our way," Gabe said. "Why don't we meet in the library train compartment and research all the dates that we have to travel to? I can brew us some coffee. Come on -- we have a lot of work to do."

Two and a half hours later, Cole and Gabe were pouring over dusty stacks of books that they had piled onto a large wooden table. They had also unrolled the scroll that Aloicius had given them and spread it out. The swirling script written on the paper said, "Save Bayard Rustin, Defeat Josephine's Cheetah, Stop Richard Lawrence, Return Samuel Adams."

Cole took a long gulp of coffee and pulled his hair in frustration. "*UGH!* Most of the moments in history that we have to fix are clearly laid out, either online or in these books; the changes that were made are easy to see. So, why can't I find anything on Bayard Rustin?"

"Same. There's nothing. Why would Bayard Rustin be considered a 'lynchpin moment' in time if there's so little information about him?" Gabe asked.

Suddenly, the door to the library compartment slid open and Brody stepped inside. His body seemed to sag from exhaustion and his face was drawn.

"Um. Hey."

"Hey," Gabe answered. There was an awkward silence.

"Do you guys need any help?"

Cole looked at him uncertainly. "I mean, sure. We'd love some help...but only if you really want to offer it."

Brody sheepishly sat down at the table and started flipping through the open books.

"Are you OK?" Gabe asked.

"I'm fine," Brody answered shortly, his eyes fixed on a book that was in front of him. He clearly didn't want to talk about what happened earlier. "So, what are you working on?"

"Well, I've been looking up stuff on Samuel Adams and Josephine Baker, and Gabe has been researching the would-be assassin Richard Lawrence," Cole explained. "We got their names from that scroll that Aloicius gave us. We've already found a lot of information. It's clear where the Master Timeline was altered for those people. For example, Josephine Baker now was imprisoned and lost everything because her cheetah killed Ernest Hemingway in 1927."

"WHAT?!" Brody cried.

"Yeah, so much of the Timeline is messed up. Samuel Adams is proving to be tricky. Just before the Boston Tea Party took place, he mysteriously vanished. Because of that, the Revolutionary War happened *completely* differently. I haven't found anything that can narrow down where he went, though. All I have so far is a random article that talks about a conspiracy theory that says that Samuel was once spotted walking around Washington D.C. in the 1830's. That sounds pretty ridiculous, though."

"Then we have Richard Lawrence who successfully assassinated Andrew Jackson," Gabe said, "which led to Martin Van Buren taking over as president earlier than he was supposed to. Spoiler alert: he led the US into a massive recession that lasted for two decades. And, finally, we have Bayard Rustin. No information at all. Neither of us have ever heard of him, so it's difficult to know where to look. It's almost like he never existed."

"Nothing on Bayard Rustin? That's odd...there should be *something,* at least. Bayard is a hugely important historical figure, after all. He helped set up the Freedom Rides and was a major organizer of the 1963 March on Washington. I mean, he was the one who taught Martin Luther King, Jr. about nonviolence! He was forced to act behind the scenes because he was gay, which seems to happen a lot in our world's history, but there should be *something* about him. Let me do some digging."

Cole watched as Brody threw himself into the research with gusto, flipping through pages and scrolling through his phone. Nostalgia burned inside his chest – it reminded him of old times.

Ten minutes later, Brody suddenly jumped to his feet.

"YES! Finally, something to go off. God, this updated Master Timeline is awful. Listen to this excerpt from *The Mechanica Brittanica:* 'The history of gay men in the 1950's is largely a punitive one. Homosexuality was illegal, and harsh punishments were meted out to anyone who was caught behaving in a way that the dominant society disliked. One example includes a man named Bayard Rustin who, after being caught committing lewd acts in a vehicle with two other men by clergyman and civil rights activist A.J. Muste, was sent to a mental hospital. He never made it out alive. This was a typical scenario of the era.' Bayard Rustin is supposed to spend time in jail, not the rest of his life in an asylum! Now, because of this change, the Civil Rights Movement happened in the 1980's, not the 1960's. Martin Luther King, Jr. never became an advocate for nonviolence. This is a disaster!"

"OK, that explains why we'll be going to the 1950's," Gabe said. "Wait...that means that we'll have to be the ones to ensure that he gets arrested now, right?" His stomach twisted uncomfortably.

"Ugh..." Brody mumbled, his face sinking. "You're exactly right. This isn't fair! What kind of mission is this? We have the power to help Bayard Rustin, maybe even make his life better than history allowed, but, instead, we're going to uphold the status quo."

"Why do you look at it like that? It's not that we're 'upholding the status quo,' Brody. The Master Timeline has unfolded in a specific way. Things happened the way that they happened for a reason," Cole said.

"For a reason? I don't know about that..."

Suddenly, random objects began pelting the sides of *The Astrolabe*. Brody walked over to a window and looked outside. An assortment of objects floated past the train: a navy blue Christian Dior dress in the "New Style" swam by the window, flapping and fluttering in the breeze; a sleek Cadillac Eldorado with dramatic tailfins roared its engine and drove off; a poster of Che Guevara bumped into a life-size model of the Russian satellite Sputnik.

49

"We're almost there," Cole said. "We'll locate Bayard, prevent A.J. Muste from forcing him into a mental asylum, and make sure that he gets taken to jail. Does that work for everyone?"

Gabe and Brody nodded in agreement.

"Let's try to do this as fast as possible. We'll get in and out and move onto the next date."

"Before we leave, can we find costumes to wear to help us blend in? The 1950's was really glamorous, so we should be able to find some fun stuff!" Brody said. They left and moved to the costume train compartment. After a few minutes, they returned wearing fedora hats, high-waisted slacks, and baggy suits with thin ties.

The Astrolabe slowed down and finally stopped in front of a white Decade Station.

"Have a great time!" Mrs. Halifax said, waving goodbye.

The boys walked off the train and Cole moved to a translucent Time Screen. He typed in the date January 21st, 1953, waited a few seconds, and then a slit unfolded in the air in front of him. The boys ran and jumped through the portal.

After sinking through the folds of time, they tumbled out of a portal and landed on the cold floor of a quaint hardware store. Assorted hand tools were displayed on rows of wooden shelves that filled the small space.

A young woman with a ponytail and cat eye glasses was standing behind a glass counter. She looked up in shock when they appeared.

"WHO ARE YOU? HOW DID YOU GET IN HERE?" she screamed.

The three boys got to their feet and scrambled out of the front door. They paused in the street and looked around.

"Umm...are we in the middle of a parade?" Cole asked.

CHAPTER SIX

The three boys jumped out of the way as a dense group of uniformed marching band members marched by, blaring their golden instruments. They looked around and saw that they had stumbled into the middle of a boisterous small-town parade. Large crowds of cheerful families mobbed the sidewalk that the boys were standing on, and bulky and brightly colored parade floats, drenched in dozens of roses and other natural elements, rolled slowly down the street: a bright yellow violin that was the size of a small car; a large duck surrounded by beautiful women wearing fluffy pastel gowns; a bright red barn that was paired with floral cows and horses. The flowers made the air smell like a heady perfume.

"Hello boys!" a flirtatious voice rang out. Cole turned his head and saw a group of high-spirited cheerleaders, dressed in long white skirts and glossy saddle shoes, smiling and waving at them.

"What is all of this?" Gabe asked.

Cole looked above the crowd's heads and spotted a line of plastic signs hanging from a rope. One of the signs read, "The Tournament of Roses."

"Looks like we landed in the middle of the Tournament of Roses Parade. That's weird, though...the parade usually happens on the first of January, but here they're doing it on the twenty-first. And at night," Cole said.

"It must be another example of the disturbances that have happened to the Master Timeline," Gabe answered.

As Brody looked through the crowd, he spotted groups of mechanicals, first generation models that were constructed out of bronze and silver plates, moving through the streets and picking up trash.

"People in the 50's can't pick up their own trash?" he grumbled.

"OK...it's just about 8:00 PM. Bayard won't be apprehended by that Muste guy until, like, 1 AM, so, unfortunately, we have several hours to kill," Cole said.

"According to our research, he's giving a speech at the Pasadena Athletic Club later tonight. I guess we can explore Pasadena a bit and then follow

Bayard when he leaves the club. He'll lead us to Mr. Muste," Gabe said.

As they made their way through the dense crowds, they overheard people commenting on the turbulent state of the sky. It churned and moved violently.

"Why does it look so strange? Is it the Reds?" a woman in a head scarf and a tweed day suit asked.

"No, it's nothing to worry about. I heard on the radio that it's just weather," a man next to her responded.

When they were finally able to break away from the heavy crowds and the hubbub of the parade, they spotted a baby blue Buick Roadmaster that was parked underneath a palm tree. Cole looked around to make sure that no one was watching before he opened the driver's side door, dug under the dashboard, and connected a few wires. The Buick Roadmaster roared to life.

"You know, that guy Nigel was a pretty terrible person, but I have to admit that he was right about this being a useful skill," he said.

The boys piled into the car, and Cole steered them down Colorado Boulevard as they headed towards the Pasadena Athletic Club. On their journey, they passed by rows of tall palm trees, dusty gas stations, and clusters of shadowy, sun-bleached buildings with Spanish arches. The wide streets that they drove down were packed with sleek and bulky cars that had large hubcaps and shiny bumpers. Off in the distance, dark mountains rose up, appearing arid and mysterious, as if the untamed world of the Wild West had never disappeared here.

Cole couldn't help but marvel at how clean and quaint Pasadena was; he felt like he had fallen into an Elia Kazan film. And, despite it being the middle of winter, the weather was dry and mild. The boys rolled down the windows and let the cool night breeze inside.

A bright light flashed at the corner of Cole's eye. When he looked in the rear-view mirror, he could see a car quickly approaching from behind.

"Who is that?" Brody wondered.

A group of teenagers in a candy apple red hot rod sped up and pulled up next to them. The song "The Glow Worm" by The Mills Brothers was playing loudly on the radio. One of the teens, a young boy with a bouffant hairstyle and a leather jacket, waved and smiled.

"Nice wheels!" said the driver of the car.

Cole laughed and waved. "Thanks!"

The driver of the hot rod leaned on the throttle, passed Cole's car, and sped down the street.

Forty minutes later, their stomachs grumbling, the boys decided to stop for dinner at a Bob's Big Boy Diner that was close to the Pasadena Athletic Club building. Neon lights lined the underside of the restaurant's flat roof, and a whimsical statue of a chubby boy wearing red-and-white overalls greeted the customers that walked in through the front doors. Several rows of bulky vehicles sat in the parking lot – it was a busy night.

When they walked inside, men and women dressed in stiff and conservative attire were moving through the diner, talking animatedly with their families or putting quarters into a jukebox. Gabe coughed and waved at the air in front of him; there was a thick haze of cigarette smoke.

The three boys slid into an empty booth with shiny vinyl seats, and they all ordered burgers and fries with a milkshake on the side. The prices were incredibly cheap.

"This tastes amazing!" Brody gushed after they had settled in and received their food. He took a large bite of his cheeseburger. "Not like the plastic fast food that we have back at Mechanica City..."

Cole smiled and sipped his strawberry milkshake, trying to ignore the discord swirling in his mind. It was nice to finally see his best friend in a good mood again, but he couldn't be sure that it would last very long.

At the back of the diner, close to the jukebox, a man in a grey fedora hat was sitting by himself and listening to a handheld radio. An authoritative voice was giving a news report, and this voice permeated throughout the diner.

"Julius and Ethel Rosenberg, convicted spies and Communist traitors, are scheduled to be

executed in June. However, there are those who are attempting to have them pardoned. Recently, film director Fritz Lang appealed to President Truman --
"

"Mommy, what's executed mean?" A little boy sitting with his mother at a nearby table stared at her with nervous eyes.

"There's nothing to worry about, honey. That's a topic for adults," his mother replied. She had her hair in short, tight curls, a poodle cut, and her red lips were a thin line of tension. She stared angrily at the man by the jukebox and barked, "Excuse me, *sir?* Turn that off! You're scaring my son."

Several pairs of tense and judgmental eyes flew to the man wearing the fedora hat. His face grew pale and he scrambled to turn off the radio. The customers in the diner returned to their food and drinks, but an air of paranoia now filled the restaurant.

"Jeez. People here are a little intense," Gabe mumbled.

After finishing their dinner, they drove over to West Walnut Street and finally arrived at the Pasadena Athletic Club. In Cole's opinion, the building looked like a multilevel stone temple from a noir film: a triangular roof; a white stone exterior; thin windows; shadowy angles and sharp edges. Cole pulled into a parking spot and turned off the car. He looked at the clock on the dashboard: 9:45 PM.

"OK, Bayard should be leaving soon," Cole said.

"Now we wait," Gabe said.

For the next twenty minutes, they sat listlessly in their seats and listened to a crooner sing ballads on the radio. Brody stretched out in the back seat and stared into space, sighing deeply every few minutes. Cole could feel that Brody's sense of irritation was increasing, but he gritted his teeth and didn't respond to it.

"You know...if we just tell Bayard not to meet up with those two guys tonight, he'll never have to go to jail at all and experience so much unnecessary trauma," Brody said after several minutes of complete silence.

"We've already talked about this, Brody," Cole answered. "If we help him avoid jail time, that will change important future events. How many times do I have to say this? Aloicius told us that the Master Timeline is only supposed to flow in a certain way."

"Yeah, well...a lot of horrible things have happened in this Master Timeline! Why shouldn't we change it? It pisses me off! Why does Aloicius get to determine what the 'true' Timeline is supposed to look like, anyway? How can we really trust him? I mean, doesn't it seem like a shame to you that we can't use *The Astrolabe* to right the wrongs of history?"

Cole didn't have a chance to offer a rebuttal because, at that moment, Bayard Rustin finally walked out of the front doors of the Pasadena Athletic Club. He was a tall and handsome black man with a big smile who was wearing a dark suit. A briefcase hung from his left hand. A group of people waved goodbye to him as he left.

"Wow. Seems like a popular guy. Come on, let's follow him," Gabe said. Cole turned the keys in the ignition and drove after him.

The hours slipped by as they followed Bayard down the quiet and dark streets of Pasadena. Cole made sure to trail several feet behind him so that Bayard didn't notice them. His movements were difficult to predict because he didn't seem to have a specific destination in mind; he was simply wandering.

A splash of twinkling stars hung above the sloping California hills, and, as the boys moved further into the night, Pasadena took on a disquieting quality. Streetlamps bathed the sidewalks in an eerie orange glow. It felt like anything could be around the next corner.

Eventually, the cheerful bounce in his step that Bayard had carried with him from earlier had melted away. Their target now seemed preoccupied and agitated. He walked slowly down sidewalks without any sense of direction. Cole felt a strange urge to hug him.

"What is he *doing?*" Gabe asked.

"He's looking for...you know. A hookup," Brody said.

"Where? On the streets?"

"I mean, I don't exactly blame him. In the 1950's, any 'activity' that was deemed sexual between homosexuals was criminalized, so meeting other gay men was nearly impossible. I can't even imagine the trauma that he lived through," Brody answered grimly.

At long last, at around one in the morning, a black car suddenly pulled up next to Bayard. He stopped to talk to the driver, leaning inside the open passenger-side window. Inside were two young white men.

"OK, here we go. *Finally,*" Brody said irritably.

Suddenly, the floor of their car began to vibrate under their feet.

"What's going on?" Cole asked nervously.

A whirring sound filled everyone's ears, and bright lights appeared in the sky, much brighter than any of the twinkling stars. Out of the darkness, three dark grey spacecrafts that were the shape of tea saucers suddenly emerged and streaked across the sky.

"*HOLY CRAP!*" Brody screamed.

The spaceships stopped and floated in mid-air, spinning in place, hovering above the boys like large postal drones. They appeared to be constructed out of a sleek metal that somehow looked both solid and liquid at the same time. Rows of tiny red lights flashed on and off along the underside of the ships.

"What the hell is that?!" Gabe screamed. He and Brody craned their necks out of the car windows, staring above them in shock and alarm. The tops of nearby palm trees bent under the pressure from the strong wind that the flying saucers were producing.

However, the moment was brief -- just as quickly as they appeared, the spaceships flew across the sky and disappeared. The wind abruptly died down and everything returned to normal again.

"What is going on – hey! Where did Bayard go?" Cole said. Their target, along with the two men, had vanished.

CHAPTER SEVEN

Cole, Brody, and Gabe stumbled out of the car and looked around wildly in all directions, desperate to catch a glimpse of the black car.

"Now we'll never find him!" Cole said in a panic. "What are we going to do?"

"I'm sorry, but can we talk about the fact that we just saw literal *aliens?!*" Brody cried.

"I...I can't even deal with that right now."

"Was Bayard *abducted?* Oh my God!"

"Wait, look over there!" Gabe said. He stepped away from their car and pointed at a trail of black splashes on the asphalt. "Do you see those oil stains? That black car must have a leaky engine. It looks like they sped away in that direction. They can't have gotten too far, let's go after them!"

With waves of stress pouring off him, Cole led them down dark streets, past quiet suburban neighborhoods and rowdy nightclubs, following the oil stains for the next ten minutes. His stomach burned with anxiety. *We can't have lost them. We just can't...*

As they turned down a side street that ran behind a row of houses, the oil stains suddenly stopped.

"No no no NO!" Cole yelled, slamming his hands on the steering wheel. "Where did the trail go?!"

"Back up! Maybe they kept going straight instead of turning. I just know that they're nearby!" Gabe urged.

Cole slammed the reverse gear down, hurriedly backed the car up, and, with a billowing cloud of dust, the Roadmaster changed directions and shot down the road.

"There!" Brody cried out.

With a massive rush of relief, Cole looked down and spotted the oil trail again – all was not lost!

"Come on...come on..." Gabe urged. He rolled down the passenger-side window and put his head out to get a better look at his surroundings. "They've got to be around here somewhere...WAIT A MINUTE! STOP!"

Cole slammed on the brakes, and they skidded to a halt near an empty parking lot that was at the back of a used car dealership.

"There it is!" Gabe whispered, pointing out of the window. The black car was parked in a shadowy parking space and the windows were fogged up.

"Um...we're not going to have to watch them hook up, right?" Cole asked.

"No, we'll just stay away from the, um, *action* until Mr. Muste arrives," Gabe answered. "And then we'll go from there."

They didn't have to wait for very long. Moments later, an elderly man wearing glasses, along with two men in white uniforms, appeared from a dark corner of the car dealership. They slowly approached the black car. One of the uniformed men was carrying a straitjacket in his hands. Cole's heart began to pound furiously in his chest.

"These guys don't look very tough. Do you think you can sneak up on them, Cole?" Gabe asked.

"Yeah, I think so. Brody, I need you to call the police and make sure they come and arrest Bayard. You can use that payphone over there."

Brody's face paled and his mouth twisted with agitation. "Um...I...."

"What is it?"

"I...I don't know if I can do that."

"What the hell are you talking about?!"

"I'm sorry!" He started wringing his hands and taking ragged breaths. "I just don't feel like I can be a part of this."

"You already agreed to help us with this, Brody!" Gabe said through gritted teeth.

"I know, but...but...this all feels wrong!"

"*But this is what happened in history!*" Cole barked. His anger was rising and he struggled to control it.

By this point, A.J. Muste and the men in white uniforms had finally reached the car. Mr. Muste threw open the passenger-side door, started shouting, and dragged Bayard out of the car. Cole's spirits dropped -- if the police didn't show up in the next few minutes, their whole plan would fall apart.

"So what?! That doesn't make it right!" Brody complained. "We don't *really* know that anything terrible will happen if we save Bayard, right? You think that I trust everything that Aloicius told us? No! Bayard didn't deserve to suffer so much in his life! Why can't we make things better?"

"BECAUSE WE CAN'T!" Cole bellowed, finally losing his patience. "You're being an idiot, Brody! Call the damn police *right now.* We're running out of time. *Just do it!*"

Brody's mouth fell open in shock. He froze, his eyes filling with angry tears.

"Oh, for God's sake, I'll do it!" Gabe cried. He marched over to the payphone, picked up the phone, and started dialing.

Cole glared at Brody and slipped the Invisibility Vambrace onto his left wrist. His body abruptly disappeared, and then he turned and strode quickly across the grass, mumbling angrily under his breath, and made his way over to A. J. Muste and the men in white uniforms.

The fog had cleared from the car windows, and Cole could see the two white men sitting inside, their faces in their hands; he felt a sharp pang of remorse in his chest. Bayard was sitting on the ground, sobbing loudly and trying to appeal to Mr. Muste.

"*Please* don't do this, A. J.," he cried. His face was twisted into a mask of pure anguish. "It won't happen again, I swear!"

"No, Bayard. You've said that to me before, and look what's happened," A. J. Muste said. He stared down at Bayard with cold distaste. "You need to admit that you've lost control of yourself. A hospital will help you. Please, come quietly and don't make a fuss."

The uniformed men grabbed Bayard's wrists, twisted his arms behind his back, and dragged him roughly to his feet. As they steered him over to their car, Cole saw his chance. He balled his hands into fists and punched the two men in the back of the head. With a low groan, they hit the ground like sacks of flour, knocked unconscious.

"Robert? George? What's the matter?!" A.J. Muste asked, looking down at the men in alarm.

Cole quietly tiptoed behind Mr. Muste, got into position, and then, with a roar, he roundhouse kicked him in the back and sent him flying across the parking lot.

Bayard threw himself against the black car, his eyes bulging in terror. "Wh-Who is there?!"

Cole froze, trying hard not to breathe too loudly.

"I know someone is there," Bayard said to the empty space in front of him, a small smile crawling up his face.

At that moment, Cole wanted to say something, *anything,* that had some weight and substance to it. Prepare Bayard for what he was about to endure. Maybe even help him escape, go somewhere that no one would bother him for being gay.

"Well...whoever you are...thank you for saving me."

Cole opened his mouth to respond, but his voice caught in his throat, and he begrudgingly stopped himself; he couldn't do that. Instead, he stayed silent and crept back to the car.

"Thanks for nothing, Brody," he said as he stomped past him. Brody was leaning against the Roadmaster with his face in his hands, but Cole was too angry to say anything else to him. He stood on the other side of the car away from Brody and crossed his arms.

Moments later, flashing lights cut through the darkness and two police cars pulled up to the parking lot, surrounding Bayard and the two men. Bright flashlight beams were shoved into Bayard's face, nearly blinding him, and he held up his hands in surrender. Handcuffs were slapped on his wrists, and then he and the two white men were led away.

Cole watched these events unfold in front of him with a heaviness in his heart. They had completed the first part of their mission, but he couldn't feel happy about this bittersweet outcome.

There was suddenly a flash of bright light. The sky stopped convulsing and returned to normal.

"I hate time travel," Brody whispered miserably. Tears rolled down his face.

"Come on...let's get out of here," Cole said gruffly. Gabe and Brody jumped into the car and they drove back to the location of the Tournament of Roses Parade.

CHAPTER EIGHT

"This is bullshit!" Brody yelled as they walked onto *The Astrolabe.* They stood in the carpeted hallway and faced off.

"What the hell is your problem? You almost ruined the mission!" Cole yelled back.

"*The mission, the mission, the mission!* That's all you ever talk about! Does the mission really take precedence over your best friend's feelings?"

"Are you *kidding me?!*" Cole bellowed. "I don't even know when these feelings of yours started! They came out of nowhere!"

Suddenly, the door that led into their train car opened and Mr. Billingsworth stepped inside. He placed a Mech-liquor tab on his tongue, swayed a little, and said, "Hello all, welcome to the --"

"NOT NOW!" Cole yelled. "Just take us to the 1920's!"

"Well. How *rude!*" Mr. Billingsworth said irritably and left the train car.

"My feelings didn't come out of nowhere!" Brody insisted. His voice was starting to quiver. "It's been like this for days! You know that I hated having to deal with that situation with Oscar Wilde. Knowing what his fate would be...talking to his friends and talking to Lord Alfred Douglas...it felt terrible! We have so much power to make things better...I'm starting to feel complicit."

"Complicit? Why would you feel like that? We didn't make the rules. We're just doing what we're told. This is so much bigger than us," Gabe said.

Brody scoffed. "Just doing what we're told? That doesn't sound very empowered or very fair, right?"

"This isn't all about you, Brody! You're being selfish. Gabe's parents and my parents have been captured! What, we're just supposed to allow them to rot in a jail cell so we can prove a point? We don't have that luxury!" Cole argued.

"Oh, like MY family hasn't been affected?!" Brody screamed. Angry tears were pouring down his face now. "*My entire family is in danger in Mechanica City!* I haven't heard from them since we left! You don't think I'm worried? It sounds like YOU'RE the selfish one!"

There was a tense pause. Cole shook with fury and indignation. Brody was making all this so much more difficult than it needed to be. Did he really think that they wanted to do any of this? What other option did they have? If they didn't complete this mission, what would Aloicius do to everyone? What would happen to all of reality?

"This isn't easy for any of us," Cole finally said.

"It's like you mentioned earlier, Brody -- if we didn't ensure that Bayard was arrested, he never would've ended up meeting Martin Luther King, Jr. and he never would've taught him about pacifism and the art of nonviolence. The Civil Rights Movement wouldn't have happened in the 1960's. If he's stuck in a mental hospital, he can't achieve any of that. Doesn't that seem worth saving? Who are we to assume that we know better and that we should mess with events that have already been put into motion?"

Brody let out a long sigh of frustration. "Obviously I don't want to change *everything*. But I'm sorry. Learning about history from a textbook versus meeting historic people in real life...seeing them as flesh and blood, with dreams and worries of their own...it's two completely different things. I know that now."

"Well...what do you want to do? Do you want to leave?" Cole asked sadly.

Brody leaned against the wall and put his face in his hands. "I...I don't know what I want to do. I'm confused..."

With a loud rushing sound, Thelonia suddenly appeared inside *The Astrolabe.* The three boys winced and shielded their eyes from the bright light that emanated from her body.

"Hello boys! You called for me?"

"What? No we didn't," Cole answered.

"Well, well, well. You're *already* set to leave, Brody? Can't handle the pressure?"

Brody blushed with embarrassment. He looked deeply flustered. "Wh-What? Well...I...I..."

"Yes? I can take you back right now if you'd like."

"No, I'm...I'm fine..."

"Are you sure?" Thelonia asked, smiling widely.

Brody nodded and stared at the floor.

"W-We're fine, Thelonia," Cole said sheepishly.

Thelonia shrugged and disappeared.

"DAMMIT!" Brody yelled. He slammed his fist against the wall. "Fine! I'll help you finish this stupid mission, OK? I mean, I'm literally being forced, so I don't have a choice. Just know that, when we finish this, I will *happily* move to New

York City so that I can finally get away from you! You will never see me again!"

Cole reeled back, feeling like he had been struck in the face. His stomach burned with anger at these painful words.

"Well...if that's what you really want..."

The Astrolabe suddenly made a low groaning sound. The three boys swayed where they stood as the train slowed down and came to an abrupt stop.

Just then, Mr. Billingsworth opened the door to their train car once again.

"So...I know that you're busy screaming at each other, but something...um...strange is in front of us," he said nervously.

"What do you mean?" Cole asked, but he didn't have to wait long to get an answer. He moved to a window and looked outside: a very large *something* was, indeed, in front of them. What that something was, though, was difficult to say. In Cole's opinion, it looked like a massive translucent wall was blocking the train's path.

"What is that thing?" Gabe asked.

"Follow me. It will make more sense from the front train compartment," Mr. Billingsworth said.

When they entered the front compartment, Mr. Billingsworth brought them over to the main control panel and had them look at a glass screen.

"Are those...?" Brody asked in a shocked whisper.

On the screen, the towering wall that blocked their way slowly came into sharper focus. It turned out to be a blockade of floating *tempesti* corpses; a mass grave stretched out ahead of them for several miles. The massive, spiked bodies were hunched over and appeared darker than the boys remembered. Their lifeless, white eyes hung open, seeing nothing.

"Oh no...those must be the dead *tempesti* that Aloicius was telling us about," Gabe said, scrunching his face in disgust.

The air seemed to go out of the train compartment. Cole suddenly felt cold and uncomfortable. These creatures were no one's favorite, especially after everything that he and his group of friends had experienced with them, but seeing this much death was deeply unsettling.

"This is disgusting," he said. "Do you think we can get by them?"

"I've never seen something like this before, so I don't know. I will try my best," Mr. Billingsworth replied.

With a flip of a switch, *The Astrolabe* powered up again and moved slowly into the sea of dead creatures. A rank smell permeated off the *tempesti* and seeped into the train, forcing the boys to hold their noses. The corpses bounced and slid against the exterior of the train with a nauseating squelching sound; a thin layer of green slime coated the windows.

"Oh, great. Now I'll have to spend hours cleaning *The Astrolabe!* As if I didn't have enough work to do," Mr. Billingsworth complained.

Cole closed his eyes and focused on his breathing so that he didn't throw up.

Ten agonizing minutes later, the train finally emerged on the other side of the corpse forest. The 1920's Decade Station could be seen off in the distance.

"Come on. Let's find some clothes in the costume compartment and get ready for Paris," Gabe said.

Mr. Billingsworth steered *The Astrolabe* towards the Decade Station.

CHAPTER NINE

Cole, Brody, and Gabe were spit out of a portal and they landed roughly on a wooden floor. They jumped to their feet and looked around at the interior of a cramped booth with a glass window. A bespectacled man wearing a stiff uniform stared at the boys in shock.

"Qui êtes-vous?" he asked.

Cole pointed his pocket watch at the man, a bright light flashed, and he crumpled to the ground.

"Nicely done, Cole!" Gabe said. "Now -- let's get started."

They stepped over the unconscious man, opened the only door in the booth, and Cole and Gabe gasped at the same time: a colossal wrought iron tower, more than a thousand feet tall, soared up to the churning blue sky above them. It was supported by four gigantic arched legs that, like the Titan Atlas, held up the mountainous lattice structure on their backs.

"WOW! Have you ever seen anything like this before?" Cole gushed.

"Well...the Chrysler Building in New York City is amazing, too. But, yeah, this is fine," Brody muttered. Cole rolled his eyes.

"Anyway...Josephine Baker is working at the Folies Bergère right now. The problem, however, is that I have no idea where that is. I forgot to look it up," Gabe said.

"Hmm...why don't we go up to the first floor of the Eiffel Tower and try and get a better look at the place?" Cole suggested. "We should be able to spot the Folies Bergère from up there. It doesn't look like there are that many stairs. Maybe a dozen?"

Unfortunately, Cole turned out to be *very* wrong about the number of stairs – there were three hundred and twenty seven, in fact. The boys were left exhausted and drenched in sweat when they finally reached the first floor of the tower. But, as they looked out at the dense, yet organized, crowd of imperious Beaux Arts-style buildings that made up the city of Paris, the intoxicating view that stared back at them made their exhaustion instantly disappear: the sprawling and illustrious Louvre Palace, the hustle and bustle coming out of the financial district, and the wide avenues bordered by horse chestnut trees.

"You know what? I take it back. The Eiffel Tower is *amazing*. I mean, look at this view!" Brody raved. He took a deep breath of the warm spring breeze blowing around them and sighed deeply.

"Look! There's the Folies Bergère building!" Cole pointed off in the distance, past a sea of white buildings, to one that was partially gold. The warm sun glinted off the surface of the Folies Bergère building and it sparkled.

"That's not too far away. Let's go!" Gabe said.

They climbed back down the long flight of iron stairs before spotting a glossy black Fiat 502 that they could hotwire. A moment later, they were enjoying the warm, floral air that poured into the open windows as they drove toward the Folies Bergère. They drove down tight, meandering roads that were bordered by long rows of white buildings. The buildings were crammed so tightly together that they were practically on top of one another. Red, white, and blue striped flags fluttered in the breeze.

As Gabe drove them further into the heart of the City of Light, Cole sat in his seat, eyes wide with excitement, and he stared hungrily out of the window at the sights of 1927 Paris: mysterious cobblestone alleyways; stone cathedrals that were decorated with menacing gargoyles; women with bobbed hair and men with straw hats. They drove over an arched bridge called the Pont de l'Alma and the boys spotted the Champs-Élysées, the Place de la Concorde, and the Palais Garnier. The dark water of the Seine River gurgled and splashed beneath them.

"By the way, what's the deal with Josephine Baker having a pet cheetah?" Gabe asked. "How did she manage that?"

"It's just one example of how fearless and *fabulous* she was," Brody replied.

On the corner of Rue St. Honore, an elderly man wearing a newsboy cap sat on a curb and played the French accordion. A small group of admirers danced to the music and laughed heartily. On every street, Paris seemed to pulse with life.

For such a large and bustling metropolis, the vibe here is so relaxed, Cole thought as he watched well-dressed and carefree people slowly strolling the sidewalks, enjoying the outdoors.

Twenty minutes later, they finally stopped in front of the Folies Bergère. The music hall was a stunning structure that resembled a white stone cube. At the center of the building's exterior was a golden bas-relief that depicted a dramatic scene of a figure leaning back, surrounded by Art Deco swirls and lines. The solid gold art piece astonished and dazzled all who gazed upon it.

They walked through a line of double doors and entered a small but dramatic lobby. The grand foyer of the Folies Bergère was brash and colorful, yet soft and regal at the same time; Brody clapped his hands over his mouth as he turned around in a circle and feasted his eyes on the sumptuous embellishments. A circular light fixture with large red candles hung directly above the foyer, bathing the carpeted floors with romantic yellow light. A second level looked down onto the blue and gold space.

The foyer was full of well-dressed men and women standing around, talking quietly with glasses of champagne in their hands. The men smoked cigars and wore tailored suits, while their sophisticated dates were draped in gorgeous, beaded flapper dresses and sparkling jewels. Cole's mind hummed with exhilaration.

The boys made their way over to a ticket window that stood underneath an awning.

"Bonjour! Je peux vous aider?" the man behind the ticket window asked. He had short, dark hair that was greased down into a middle part, and he paired it with a thin, pencil moustache.

"Umm...no francais," Gabe answered sheepishly.

A sour expression rolled across the mustachioed man's face. "What do you want?" he huffed.

"We would like three tickets to, um, the 'Danse Sauvage.' The show with Josephine Baker," Cole said.

The man handed them their tickets and they gave him some money.

"Oh, before we go into the theater, I wanted to check on Karma and Ruby," Cole said to Gabe and Brody, and he stepped to the side, away from the ticket window, and took out his portable radio.

"Karma? Are you there?"

There was nothing but static.

"Karma? Hello? How is everything going?"

He repeated himself a few more times, but no one answered.

"Hmm. Maybe she and Ruby are busy," Gabe suggested.

"Yeah. Maybe..." Cole replied. "I'll try her again later."

The boys crossed the grand foyer and walked up a short flight of stairs that led into the theater. A wall of sound greeted them when they entered the music hall. The theater had three levels, and the air was filled with loud chatter from a crowd of at least two hundred people crammed into rows of seats, as well as upbeat jazz music that an unseen band was playing. The carpet was crimson red.

Cole looked to his left and spotted a glossy wooden bar. He was suddenly reminded of the famous painting *A Bar at the Folies-Bergère* by Édouard Manet.

"Wanna get drinks before the show?" he asked. "I mean, we're at the Folies Bergère! We might as well take advantage of that fact. And besides, I'm going to need a drink to get through this task."

After the boys bought glasses of red wine, they moved to three seats near the front of the stage and sat down.

"OK, let's go over our plan again," Gabe said. "As soon as we see Chiquita the cheetah, what will you do, Cole?

"I'll hit her with a tranquilizer dart."

"Exactly. She won't get hurt, but it will knock her out for a few hours. That should give Ernest Hemingway plenty of time to avoid getting eaten by the wild animal. And Brody? You can just, you know, watch everything happen."

"What a treat," Brody grumbled.

"Now, the audience will probably start to panic when Chiquita goes down, so, as soon as that happens, we'll just blend in with the crowd and sneak out. Done and done!"

A trumpet flourish sounded, and the unseen band kicked the tempo up a notch as the revue finally began. A line of sparkling chorus girls whooped and cheered as they danced onto the stage in front of the curtain. Cole was shocked to see that they were all nearly nude, with their translucent sequin bras and underwear leaving little to the imagination. Colorful feathers moved and fluttered under the hot stage lights as the dancer's lithe bodies twirled across the stage. They formed a line and kicked out their long legs at the same time, causing the audience to clap and cheer appreciatively. The chorus girls winked and smiled at the audience.

As soon as their number was finished, the bawdy chorus girls rushed off the stage and they were replaced by a man and woman who performed acrobatic stunts. Clad in tight outfits that clung to their bodies, they moved about the stage and completed complex choreography. At one point, the woman leaped into the air and landed feet-first on the man's shoulders; the crowd responded with *oohs* and *aahs*. Then, she did a back flip and landed on the ground. She thrust her hands into the air and Cole, Gabe, and Brody rose to their feet and cheered along with the rest of the audience.

When the acrobats exited the stage, the lights suddenly faded to black and low drumbeats rolled through the music hall. Everyone in the audience exchanged looks of excitement and anticipation.

The red curtain finally rose, and the stage transformed into a lush jungle scene. Large green leaves and thick ivy hung above an enormous tree branch that stretched across the stage. Black actors in loin cloths slowly emerged from the wings, swinging their arms and moving to the music.

Suddenly, from the left side of the stage, a gorgeous young black woman began to slink across the top of the tree branch. A skirt of artificial bananas hung from her shapely waist, and finger waves rippled through her glossy black hair. The moment that she appeared onstage, the audience raised their glasses and cheered enthusiastically. Cole blushed deeply at the sight of her exposed breasts.

Josephine Baker shook her hips erotically from side to side and dominated the cabaret hall with her massive energy and charisma – she held everyone in the palm of her hands. In that moment,

Cole was keenly aware that he was in the presence of a world-famous talent at the top of their game, and it was mesmerizing.

As the performance continued, Cole spotted the cheetah named Chiquita. She slowly entered the stage and laid down by the wings; the audience gasped and chuckled at the sight of her. The gorgeous animal licked her paws and watched the performance.

"Get the tranquilizer dart ready," Gabe whispered.

Now was Cole's chance: he slowly lifted the tranquilizer gun, aimed, and pressed the trigger. A long dart shot out of the barrel, flew slightly to the right, and lodged itself into the stage floor, missing the target completely. Chiquita opened her wide jaws and roared in surprise. She jumped down into the orchestra pit and the audience laughed and cheered.

Cole flushed with anger and kicked himself internally. *Dammit, dammit, dammit!*

The bananas around Josephine's waist fluttered and moved as she continued to thrust her hips and dance around the stage. Just before the number ended, she crossed her eyes and made silly facial expressions before finishing in the splits. The audience erupted in loud applause and jumped to their feet.

"Well...what do we do now?" Gabe asked.

"I don't know. I don't see Chiquita anywhere," Cole answered.

"I mean...I might have an idea," Brody said.

"You do?" Cole asked.

"We'll have to ingratiate ourselves with Josephine, though," Brody answered. "We'll need to locate her and somehow convince her to take us out to a café. All the research stated that she's going to one with friends after this performance, and that's where Chiquita attacks Ernest."

"Hmm...that's not a bad idea. But how will we find her?" Cole asked.

"I spotted a door that leads backstage. We can try to find her dressing room."

"You want us to sneak backstage? I don't know..."

"This plan is totally crazy, but it seems like it's our only option now," Gabe said. "Besides, Cole, don't you want to meet Josephine Baker?!"

As the crowd began to file out of the cabaret hall, Cole and Gabe followed Brody to the side of the stage. In the corner, they could just make out a door that led backstage. A gruff man was guarding the entrance.

"Shall I do the honors?" Gabe asked, slipping the Invisibility Vambrace onto his wrist.

"Good luck," Cole whispered.

Gabe vanished. Then, he moved behind the man that was guarding the entrance, stuck him with a tranquilizer dart, and he sank to the floor.

"Follow me!" Brody said, and they made their way backstage.

The backstage area of the Folies Bergère was a dusty, wooden labyrinth. The three boys made their way around tight corners and down crowded hallways, passing by colorful set pieces and thin curtains with large tears in them. At one point, a gaggle of half-naked chorus girls ran by them.

"Brody, do you have any idea where we're going?" Gabe asked as they walked down an empty corridor.

"Well, the star of the show usually has their own dressing room, and it will be the biggest one.

Josephine Baker is the biggest star to ever headline the Folies Bergère, so her room is bound to be huge and obvious. It's got to be around here somewhere...Look! Here we are!" Brody said. They approached a door with a yellow paper star attached to it and knocked.

The door opened and a stern-looking black woman answered the door. She had light brown skin and was wearing a green straight-line chemise dress. A lit cigar rested in her hand. Chiquita the cheetah was curled up in the corner.

"What do you want?" the woman asked.

Over her shoulder, the boys could see Josephine Baker sitting at a dressing table. She was wearing a lilac silk robe and silver earrings.

"We-We need to speak with Miss Baker," Cole said.

"Miss Baker isn't seeing anyone at the moment, especially not uninvited guests," the woman said austerely.

"But...But it's urgent! We, um, want to write her biography and we *must* interview her," Brody explained, blurting out the first thing that came to his mind.

"Well, she ain't interested!" the woman barked, and she made to shut the door.

"Oh, it's fine, Bricktop!" Josephine said cheerfully. "I love anyone who wants to write about me."

"But we're just about to go out," Bricktop lamented.

"It won't take longer than a minute. Will it, boys?"

Cole, Brody, and Gabe nodded enthusiastically.

"Oh, don't give me that look. Come here, Bricky," Josephine purred, and she beckoned with her finger. Bricktop smiled, moved over to her, and the two women kissed deeply for several seconds. When they were finished, Bricktop left the dressing room. The three boys smirked and looked at the floor.

"Don't look so shocked, now," Josephine teased the boys. "I'm an equal opportunity lover. Men, women...I like a little bit of everything!"

Floral perfume wafted in the air as she walked by them. She stepped behind a folding screen and began to remove her clothes.

"Don't worry. We're all gay, so it's not shocking," Brody said.

"Ooh! How chic!" Josephine said.

She emerged from behind the folding screen wearing an orange beaded shift dress and a fur trimmed coat, and then sat back down at her dressing table to touch up her makeup.

"So. Who are you boys?"

"I'm Cole, and this is Brody and Gabe," Cole replied.

"And you want to write a book about my life, is that right?"

"Yes. We're big fans!"

"Who do you work for? I need a little more information."

Cole suddenly went quiet and didn't know what to say. He looked to Brody for help.

"We work for, um, Random House, the publishing company. We're all very interested in writing a biography of you," Brody answered.

Josephine giggled and lit a cigarette. She took a long drag and blew the smoke into the air.

"Why do you wanna write a book about me? I haven't really done anything yet."

"What are you talking about? You're sensational! The most popular black artist in France right now! That's quite an accomplishment."

"Would anyone read it, though? I haven't exactly made it in America yet."

"That doesn't matter!" Brody insisted. "You have a lot of fans, Miss Baker. I mean, you can see the huge audiences that show up for you. You're a boundary breaker! And we'll help market the book to as wide an audience as possible."

Cole nodded encouragingly.

"Yeah. We'll make sure that it sells! We have many contacts through Random House," Gabe said.

Josephine thought for a moment, refreshing her lipstick in the mirror.

"Well...you're lucky that you're cute, because you've convinced me!" she finally said. "So, how do you want to do this? What do I have to do?"

"All you have to do is, um, answer a few of our questions," Brody explained.

"Well, like Bricktop mentioned, I'm on my way to meet some friends now. How about you come with us? You can interview me then!"

"We'll do it!" Brody said.

CHAPTER TEN

"Where are we going?" Cole asked.

The three boys followed Josephine, Bricktop, and Chiquita down a flight of rickety wooden stairs. Brody kept glancing at the cheetah nervously.

"The Café de Flore, my dears!" Josephine said. "One of the most fabulous cafés in Paris. You will love it! My friend Ernest is waiting for us."

As soon as they stepped out of the Folies Bergère stage door, a group of men wearing dark suits and fedora hats mobbed them. Bright camera flashes popped in the air as the photographers hungrily snapped pictures of Josephine.

"Regarde ici!"

"Souris à la caméra!"

"Bonjour, mes garçons!" Josephine said with a big, toothy smile. She placed her hands on her hips and struck several glamorous poses.

Cole, Gabe, and Brody quietly started to panic, and they pulled their bowler hats down over their eyes so that the photographers couldn't capture them – they weren't supposed to exist during this time period, after all. Luckily, hiding wasn't difficult to accomplish; the photographers only wanted shots of Josephine, anyway.

Chiquita tugged on her leash and roared loudly at the photographers.

"Alright, that's enough! Little Miss Chiquita is feeling grumpy. You boys better come see me in the show, now!" Josephine said. She followed Bricktop to a Rolls Royce Phantom limousine that was parked on the sidewalk. It was white, with a uniformed driver and an open roof. Everyone piled in and the driver took off.

"So...have y'all ever been to Paris before?" Bricktop asked.

"No, this is our first time," Brody answered. "We came all the way here just to interview Miss Baker! She's a fascinating person."

Josephine blushed and giggled. "Oh, call me Josephine. And, my goodness, your first time? We must celebrate! Bricktop, could you pass me the drink?"

Bricktop reached under the seat and pulled out a large bottle of expensive champagne. She held the bottle out of the car and popped the cork; it flew off into the distance. Bricktop and Josephine whooped with laughter, and everyone clinked their glasses together in celebration.

For the next thirty minutes, the driver drove them through the charming city. Cole couldn't believe that such a beautiful place really existed. As they drove down the winding and tight cobblestone streets, Chiquita's head resting in his lap, he felt like he was in a dream.

"So, how did you get the nickname Bricktop?" Gabe asked.

"Well, when I lived in Chicago and was coming up with saloon folks, they noticed my red hair and freckles, so they called mc Bricktop," she answered. "My birth name is Ada. Ada Smith."

"You worked at a saloon in Chicago? Fascinating!" Brody exclaimed. "We'll have to include you in our biography of Josephine."

"Oh, you must! Bricktop has so many good stories. She knows everybody," Josephine said. "And I mean *everybody*. She's the doyenne of café society! Anyone who is anyone goes to her nightclub, the Chez Bricktop."

"Scott Fitzgerald, Cole Porter, everybody!" Bricktop said.

Cole, Gabe, and Brody exchanged shocked glances. Bricktop's list of famous names made them dizzy with excitement!

"I LOVE PARIS!" Josephine suddenly shouted out, and she laughed and stood up in the back seat of the car. She held her arms out as the wind moved through her dress -- she was glorious. Bricktop giggled and pulled her back down to her seat.

The driver eventually stopped in front of a café that was positioned on the corner of Boulevard Saint-Germain and Rue Saint-Benoit. A large awning with the words Café de Flore, written in swirling black script, hung over the main entrance. On top of the awning rested a thick cluster of brightly colored flowers; Cole took a deep breath and inhaled their floral scent. In front of the café, taking up most of the sidewalk, were several groupings of tables and chairs.

"Thank you so much, Hugo!" Josephine said as she stepped out of the car, Chiquita in tow. She planted a kiss on the driver's cheek and he blushed deeply.

A handsome man with a dark moustache and a black beret suddenly walked out of the Café de Flore and approached them. He was tall, with broad shoulders and a strong jaw, and there was a confident swagger to his walk. Cole's heart began to race when he recognized the famous novelist.

"Josie! Bricktop! You made it!" the man said. He hugged the two women tightly.

"Hello Papa! Gentlemen, this is my good friend Ernest Hemingway," Josephine said.

"Who are these people? You didn't tell me that anyone else was joining," Ernest said. He stared pointedly at the three boys.

"These are some new friends that I met on my way here. Ernest, meet Cole, Brody, and Gabe. They want to work on a project with me," Josephine explained. "But not to worry, these boys are lovely. Come on, let's grab a table outside."

Everyone moved to a circular table that was standing on the sidewalk off by itself. Waiters wearing black vests and white aprons bustled around them and took their orders. They smiled widely and acted like perfect supplicants, paying special attention to Josephine because of her fame.

"I thought that Gertrude and Jean would be joining us?" Bricktop said, puffing on a cigar.

"That was the original plan, but Jean is stuck working on his opera-oratorio and we all know how Gertrude is. Pablo stopped by her studio and they got to talking about, and, eventually, painting the sky. Apparently, she's lost all track of time."

"Jean? Gertrude?" Brody asked.

"Jean Cocteau and Gertrude Stein," Ernest answered.

Brody choked on his wine.

The waiters in white aprons came around once again and served them glass carafes of rich coffee, porcelain plates piled high with buttery croissants and finger sandwiches, and all the red wine that they could drink – Josephine paid for all of it. Sitting with three stars of the age, taking in the mild spring weather, Cole felt like his mind was humming.

"Now, let's talk about that book," Josephine said. "What would you like to know first?"

Brody took the lead. "Well, let's start with your childhood. Can you tell us where you were born?"

"I was born in St. Louis, Missouri."

"What was your experience like? Did you enjoy it there?"

Josephine chuckled. "Oh no. No, it was *very* difficult. Me and my mama were dirt poor. I lived on the streets for many years. Sometimes I even danced on street corners. And I didn't do half bad! It helped put food on the table sometimes. And I discovered my talent for dancing by going through that."

"Was your mother able to help with the bills?" Gabe asked.

"She did her best." Josephine paused for a moment, her eyes becoming glassy and distant. "She would take in laundry sometimes. I...well. Anyway. Things were tough for a very long time, but we got through it."

Ernest refilled her wine glass and held her hand gently. Josephine wiped a tear from her eye.

"What were your parents like? Were you close?" Cole asked.

"Well...I never knew my father, but my mama is nice enough. She doesn't like what I do for a living, though, so we don't talk much now. She just wants me to get married, but I've done it twice already and it wasn't much to write home about, I can tell you that."

Brody drained his glass and shook his head in shock. The wine was making him relaxed and talkative. "I'm *so* sorry that you experienced that! And at such a young age? You've already overcome so much in your life."

"Well, no more than other folks, I guess."

"Josephine, can I ask you a question?"

She chuckled. "You can ask me as many as you want!"

"I'm curious...do you ever wish that it had been easier for you when you were growing up?"

"Oh, no. Definitely not," Josephine said matter-of-factly.

"Really? Why not?"

"Well, what would be the point in that? The only way through this life is forward, not backwards. I ain't a victim. I live my life with no regrets!"

Next to Josephine, Bricktop nodded in agreement, put down her cigar, and held up her wine glass. Everyone cheered and clinked their glasses together.

"That's great! But, I mean, let's say you actually *could* change the past," Brody pressed. "Wouldn't you want to do that?"

"I don't think so, no. I've learned something from every difficult time in my life. How do you think I got street smarts?"

Brody lapsed into silence. He stared into space, thinking deeply.

"Now, I wanted to ask you something. I want to be truthful about my life, but I've got some tough stories that might...you know...make some white folks in America uncomfortable. Let's just say that there's a reason why I'm in Paris, OK?"

"We completely understand," Brody said. "That's actually one of the reasons why we wanted to talk to you! You have a unique lived experience and perspective."

"What publishing house did you say that you work for?" Ernest asked. He took a gulp of his wine.

"Random House," Cole answered.

"Huh. Well, Scribner's published me last year. I'm sure you've heard of my novel. *The Sun Also Rises?* It's already been printed twice, you know."

"I'm sure these boys know all about your novel, Ernest," Josephine said, smirking.

"So, if you ever need any help with the writing, I'm available." Ernest smiled and drank deeply from his wine glass again.

"We'll keep that in mind," Gabe replied.

For the next hour, Ernest drank heavily while he abruptly steered the conversation to bullfighting. As he launched into a long monologue about a man who had (seemingly) wronged him, his face became flushed and sweaty.

"The brute thought that he could win against me in a fight! *HA!* Well, he learned a lesson that day. But a-anyway, that reminds me of the Festival of San Fermin. Have any of you heard of it? It's in P-Pamplona. I saw my first bullfight there in 1923. Quite marvelous. The energy was breathtaking. Man against beast. A true test of strength!"

"I've seen a bullfight," Cole said.

"You have? What did you think?" Ernest asked.

"I saw one in Mexico City. It, um, wasn't my favorite."

"Huh. Well...you need a strong stomach to enjoy it. Besides, the bull fights in Pamplona are much better. I don't put much stock in Mexico City. When I go to Pamplona again, you and your friends must join me. It is an experience that will ch-change your life!"

He took more gulps from his wine glass and playfully reached for Chiquita's tail. She growled at him.

"Oh, Ernest. You better stop doing that, she doesn't like being teased. She's a lot like me in that way," Josephine warned.

Cole exchanged nervous glances with Brody and Gabe – this was the moment that they had been waiting for.

"It's fine! You don't think I can handle a beast like this?" He laughed loudly and reached for her tail again. Chiquita pulled it away, roared loudly, and swatted at him with her large paws.

"Ernest..." Bricktop cautioned.

Ernest finally caught Chiquita's tail and pulled; the cheetah let out a terrible roar and scrambled to her feet. As she leaned back and prepared to rip Ernest's throat out, Cole acted quickly. He pulled out the tranquilizer gun, aimed, and fired at Chiquita. The dart sank into her furry shoulder, and she dropped to the sidewalk. Everyone jumped to their feet in a panic.

"What the hell did you do that for?" Bricktop screamed at Cole.

"She was going to kill Ernest!" he cried.

"You just happened to have a tranquilizer dart in your pocket?"

"Um...yeah. You don't carry one?"

Chiquita slowly stumbled to her feet and roared groggily. She swayed from side to side, crashing into nearby tables and sending glassware flying. No one could tell what she was going to do. Cars on the street screeched to a halt to watch what would happen.

"Calm down, Chiquita!" Josephine cried.

The cheetah looked at her in a daze and then took off running. People strolling down the sidewalk jumped out of the way as she headed straight for them. Chiquita knocked into trash cans and slammed into chairs as she lumbered down the sidewalk.

"CHIQUITA! COME BACK!" Bricktop cried, and everyone ran after the fleeing animal.

Chiquita swerved to the left and crossed into traffic. A Ford Model T narrowly avoided the frightened animal by swerving out of the way. A crowd of people screamed and pointed as they watched the chaos unfold.

"WATCH OUT!" Cole screamed as he ran down the street, knocking passersby out of the way; the rest of the group was in hot pursuit. A wave of panic nearly bowled him over. If they didn't stop Chiquita soon, a police officer would surely shoot her. He dug in his pocket and loaded the tranquilizer gun with a dart – his last one. There was no room to miss.

As Chiquita ran down an avenue, she accidentally tripped over her paws and slammed into the side of a baguette shop. The glass on the front window smashed all over the sidewalk. The cheetah slumped to the ground and fell unconscious, the effects of the tranquilizer dart finally taking hold. Cole and the rest of the group skidded to a halt in front of her.

"Oh, my darling!" Josephine cried. She ran to the unconscious cheetah. "Je suis désolé, my friends! Chiquita is a good girl. She is not usually like this!"

"You idiot! I told you not to bother her!" Bricktop yelled at Ernest.

Ernest's face was pale and he looked sheepish. "Well, I...I was just messin around! What can I say? Animals usually love me. But look, no harm done! Chiquita is fine."

"No harm done? Look at the damage that mon petit ange caused!" Josephine yelled.

Ernest stared at the overturned furniture and the glass shards littering the sidewalk.

"Well...OK. You're right. I was being foolish. I'm very sorry, I must have had too much to drink."

"You most certainly were being foolish," Bricktop scolded.

There was a flash of bright light and the Parisian sky suddenly returned to normal.

"Thank you for saving my life." Ernest moved to Cole and shook his hand. He had a very firm grip. "Let me make it up to all of you. Drinks on me?" He flashed his handsome smile to the group.

Josephine still looked angry, but she quickly relented – Ernest Hemingway's charm was too difficult to resist. "Well...alright, you scoundrel. But, as punishment, I'm going to make you carry Chiquita to the next café!"

Cole, Gabe, and Brody looked at each other excitedly -- they had done it! Ernest Hemingway was saved.

"Well...I think this might be a good time for us to leave," Brody said.

"Oh, you can't! I barely told you anything about me," Josephine cried.

"I'm really sorry, Miss Baker, but we're very busy and have other business to attend to. Here is our telephone number. We will have our agent reach out to you with more information about the book as soon as we start writing it, but you can call us at any time!"

Brody wrote down a fake number on a piece of paper and handed it to Josephine. He felt a twinge of remorse for lying to her, but the feeling quickly disappeared when he remembered that she would have dozens of biographies written about her by the time that she passed away in 1975.

"Magnifique! It was lovely to meet all of you!" Josephine said.

The three boys smiled, turned around, and headed back to the Eiffel Tower.

CHAPTER ELEVEN

The sky, a violent shade of crimson, churned and convulsed above Mechanica City. It looked down upon the dysfunction and chaos that continued to plague the metropolis. The roads and bridges were severely cracked and damaged, so traversing the city was nearly impossible for many of its citizens, and several city blocks of office buildings and apartments burned steadily.

Inside Arthur's manor house, Ruby had stationed herself inside the living room. Two days had passed since she and Karma had arrived, and they had pushed aside overturned pieces of furniture, boarded up the windows, and carved out a space to think and strategize. There was so much work to be done and plans to be made, and all of it had to be figured out with barely any preparation time at all.

Ruby, her legs curled underneath her on a squishy armchair, was typing furiously on her laptop. The laptop screen was covered with articles concerning Gustav Fallowback; she had at least fifteen different tabs open. His birth certificate, high school records, the deed to his house on Shubert Street -- she wanted to learn everything that she possibly could about the monster that had changed her life.

She winced and massaged her temple; for the past hour, a sharp headache had bloomed over her left eye. The idea of taking a break or relaxing was laughable to her, but she couldn't deny that her research was starting to negatively affect her. Her eyes burned from staring at her laptop for so long, and her back was riddled with tension.

Her eyes suddenly fell across an article that had been written ten years ago. It was a feature on Gustav and his work with the patent office at Bennett Industries. In a photograph that was posted with the article, Gustav could be seen handing an award to local engineering celebrity Magnus Everard. His (former) high standing in the Mechanica City engineering community was evident.

The old man in the photograph looked smug and cantankerous. Wispy tufts of white hair sprouted from the top of his head, and the skin on his cheeks drooped and sagged. As Ruby stared at Gustav's haggard face, his yellow smile sent chills down her spine. Her hands began to shake, and she broke out into a cold sweat as an uncontrollable wave of thorny memories pierced her mind: the burning sensation on her cheek after Jaxon hit her for the first time; a circle of cruel strangers surrounding her and laughing; emerging from a comfortable slumber, only to find herself confused and frightened all over again. The memories came rapidly and brought tears to her eyes. She slammed the laptop shut and took several deep breaths.

Suddenly, Karma rushed into the room. She had a cell phone pressed to her ear and her eyes blazed with fire.

"Oh my God, you don't know how grateful I am! I mean, you're actually ready to meet? Today?" she asked.

Ruby perked up in her chair with curiosity. She could hear someone's voice mumbling on the other end of the line.

After several "Uh huh's" and "OK, great's," Karma smiled widely and hung up.

"What is it?"

"I *finally* have some good news! Do you remember when I told you about my friend John? The one who had a cousin who worked under Gustav several years ago?"

"Yes, I think so."

"Well, I finally tracked him down. It took some convincing, but he agreed to talk to us. He says that he can tell us how to find Gustav!"

"Are you serious? That's amazing!"

"I've known him for a long time, so I trust him. If he says that he has information, he has information. John wants to meet us at a bowling alley called Solid 8. Let's go!"

"A bowling alley?" Ruby asked in disbelief.

"Yeah, it's a bit strange, but it's such a random place that no one would think to look for us there. It's so far out that it's practically in Scuz, so we'd better get going."

"Can't he just text you the information that he has?"

"No, it's too dangerous. Someone could be tracking his phone. We don't know how strong Project Hominum still is."

An uncomfortable mixture of anxiety and anticipation filled Ruby's stomach. For the past two days, she and Karma had been trying desperately to get a lead on any information concerning Gustav; he was a difficult man to track down. Now, after sleepless nights and hours of research, they were finally on track to getting some answers. Would they find what they were looking for?

Ruby slowly got to her feet. She picked up her blaster, stuck it in her boot, pulled on a heavy jacket, and followed Karma out of the front door.

Karma led Ruby down broken cobblestone streets with deep gashes in them. The streets were empty and eerie – most of the Mechanica City citizens were hiding inside their homes.

"So...this John guy's cousin used to work for Gustav?" Ruby asked.

"John isn't actually his real name, but yes, that's right. I've known him for a few years, and he knows everything that goes on in this city -- nothing gets past him. If there's anyone who can help us track down Gustav, it's John. According to his cousin, Gustav has gone into hiding, but she discovered the location."

"Good. Let's finally get that bastard," Ruby said. Gustav and Project Hominum were the cause of all their pain, and it was time to punish them once and for all.

Mechanica City was even more difficult to navigate now because of the various time changes that had occurred. Buildings and landmarks had either disappeared or were in a different location. Not only that, but everything was now more dangerous. The two women passed by a high school building that was engulfed in flames. Bright orange fire climbed up the walls of the brick structure; Karma and Ruby coughed from the acrid smoke in the air.

At a four-way stop, they paused to watch a group of men and women loot a grocery store. A middle-aged man smashed a window with a hammer and a horde of looters poured inside, stealing whatever they could get their hands on. Despite their disgust and sadness, Ruby and Karma put their heads down and continued walking. They had seen this exact same scenario play out several times over the past few days. There was nothing to be done.

Suddenly, the raging sky above them convulsed, and a bright blast of lightning rained down and struck the street. Ruby and Karma screamed and fell to the ground.

"How the hell did that happen?" Ruby asked.

"I...I don't know, but let's keep moving," Karma answered. Her voice was small and it shook nervously.

Karma and Ruby continued walking the streets, feeling hardened but focused. They were all alone, and the world around them had collapsed. There was no way to be sure of anything. All they had now was blind faith.

"So...I have a question for you," Karma said as she climbed over a large pile of rubble. She grabbed Ruby's hand and helped her over it.

"What is it?"

"When we eventually find Gustav, I plan to...um...eliminate him. If you catch my meaning. How do you feel about that?"

Unease flickered across Ruby's mind. She had thought about this question many times but had never settled on a definitive answer. However, it was important for her to show Karma that she was strong. Karma had risked her life to accompany her on this journey, so Ruby kept her face neutral.

"Well...I-I don't know. Gustav deserves to be severely punished, of course. Taking him out is the smartest thing to do."

"Good. So, you agree."

"However, I have so many questions that I need to ask him. Getting answers is still a priority for me."

"Oh, of course! But what if Gustav refuses to answer them?" Karma asked. "According to John's cousin, he doesn't take well to questioning and is extremely stubborn. It may be difficult to get anything out of him."

"But...Jaxon is dead. Gustav is my only opportunity to get closure," Ruby answered. "I have to try. Besides, we *could* always detain him and make sure he rots in prison for the rest of his miserable life. That is an option."

"A horrific man like him? The reason for all our pain and misery?! Prison is too good..." Karma said.

Twenty minutes later, Karma led Ruby down a narrow alleyway and they finally came upon Solid 8. The shattered windows were dark and empty and rats skittered away from their feet. Perched on top of the small, brick bowling alley was a neon sign that was in the shape of a bowling pin.

"Well...we made it," Karma said.

As they approached the bowling alley, she turned around abruptly to look behind them. A chill rolled down her spine – someone, or something, had just knocked against a nearby dumpster. However, after several seconds, when no one approached them, she and Ruby continued walking.

"Are you sure this is the right place?" Ruby asked in disbelief. She was starting to have second thoughts.

"Yes, this is the address. Come on, let's go inside."

Karma grabbed a handle on the front door and pulled – it was locked.

"Now what?" Ruby wondered.

Looking around, Karma spotted a broken window on the right side of the brick building. She ran, dove through the window, and landed feet-first inside a tiled entrance lobby. Then, she opened the front door and let Ruby inside.

They walked through the entrance lobby before stepping into the dark bowling alley. At the back of the large room, several rows of greased bowling lanes stretched out in front of them. A black pinsetter with spindly arms was positioned at the back of the bowling lanes, a metal monster that stood guard over the pins. Wooden beams crisscrossed the ceiling, and dark light fixtures hung from them.

As they slowly approached the rows of bowling lanes, they strode by a wooden bar with shelves that held numerous dusty liquor bottles. Ruby eyed the bottles enviously – she could really use a drink right now.

Suddenly, the sound of crunching glass came from a dark corner. Karma and Ruby turned and pointed their blasters.

"Who is there?" Karma barked.

A man slowly stepped out of the shadowy corner. He was middle-aged, and he had a dark beard and curly brown hair. He wore a dark trench coat with the lapel pulled up to his ears.

"Karma. It's been a long time," he said. His voice was shaky and faint.

"It has," Karma replied, her chin wobbling. They walked up to each other and embraced.

"John, this is, um, my associate Ruby."

"Nice to meet you," she said.

"It's so good to see you again. You don't know how much I appreciate you meeting with us," Karma said.

John nodded briefly. He pressed a button on his watch.

"So...I believe you have something that we're looking for?" Karma asked.

"Umm yes. B-But we can't talk down here. There is a better area upstairs."

"Of course. Lead the way."

Ruby and Karma followed the informant up a nearby staircase that creaked and groaned underneath their steps.

"So...a lot has happened since we last spoke. How is your wife?" Karma asked pleasantly.

"Oh, Amber's fine. Really good...everything is good."

He led them down a short hallway and into a bare office. The only piece of furniture in the room was a wooden desk. A row of windows looked down onto the bowling alley below.

"And how are your kids?"

John stood stiffly in the middle of the room. He nervously picked at a spot on his cheek.

"They're...fine."

"What has it been? A year since we last spoke?"

John didn't answer. He stared at the floor in silence.

Karma and Ruby looked at each other with confused expressions. John started wringing his hands.

"OK...? Well, I guess we'll get right to it," Karma said. "What information do you have about Gustav Fallowback's whereabouts?"

John abruptly burst into tears. He brought his hands up to his face and sobbed loudly, tears pouring down his cheeks.

"Wh-What's the matter?" Karma asked nervously.

"I'm so sorry, Karma. I didn't want to do this."

"What are you talking about?"

"They're...They're making me do it. They have Amber and the kids."

"Wait a minute. Who has her?" Ruby asked, panic rising in her throat.

They could suddenly hear heavy footsteps running up the stairs.

"He means Project Hominum!" Karma cried.

"*You betrayed us!*"

"Is that true, Benjamin?!" Karma asked, revealing her informant's real name.

An armed Project Hominum guard kneeled at the top of the staircase and suddenly opened fire, striking Benjamin in the legs and shoulder. He screamed as his body flailed wildly, dark red blood spraying across the walls of the bare office, and he collapsed to the ground.

"Come out of there!" the guard screamed. They pressed the mouthpiece on their face mask. "Hey, this is Carson. I need back up!"

Seconds later, more guards thundered up the stairs. Karma and Ruby screamed and hid on either side of the doorway.

"We're trapped!" Ruby cried.

"No, we're not! We can still get out of this. Just start firing!" Karma said.

With their blasters held in the air, they turned and fired off several rounds at the group of guards. Some of their shots missed and blew holes in the surrounding walls, sending chunks of plaster and wood flying across the floor. Others, however, reached their targets, striking two of the guards squarely in the chest. They cried out in pain and fell to the floor.

A barrage of bullets flew back at them. Ruby screamed and hid behind the wall again, her heart pounding in her chest.

"Stay focused!" Karma bellowed.

When the first guard pushed their way into the office, she sprang into action. She grabbed them by the throat, lifted them off the ground, and slammed them against a wall -- a deep dent was left in the plaster. The guard groaned and sank to the floor.

The last three guards ran into the room, and a chaotic fistfight broke out. While Karma kicked a guard in the stomach, Ruby was pushed towards the wall as she ducked away from her assailant's fists. She tried to put the desk in between them, but the guard moved too fast.

"RACE TRAITOR!" the guard screamed. With a loud cry, they rushed towards her, hands balled into fists. However, at the last second, Ruby dove to the floor and rolled out of the way – her blaster fell out of her hands. The guard smashed through the row of windows and, with a scream, fell to the bowling alley below.

"HUMANS FIRST!" screamed a tall guard that was brawling with Karma.

"Oh, SHUT UP!" she roared back, punching them in the face.

Undeterred, the guard reached forward and roughly thrust their palm into Karma's neck. She grabbed her throat, gasping for air, and sank to her knees.

"KARMA!" Ruby screamed.

The guard pulled their blaster out and pointed it at her. "Time's up, you filthy robot."

Adrenaline pumping fiercely in her head, Ruby scrambled for her fallen blaster, aimed, and fired – an energy blast shot out and hit the guard in the back. They collapsed to the ground.

"B-Behind you!" Karma gasped, hacking and coughing. But it was too late -- the last remaining guard struck Ruby on the back of the head. Stars popped in front of her eyes and she collapsed.

Ruby slowly raised her head, her vision blurry, and watched as her friend screamed with a fiery rage. Something seemed to have snapped inside Karma, and she viciously attacked the final Project Hominum guard. Leaping into the air, she kicked out her leg and slammed her foot right into their face. After landing on the ground, she then spun around, performed a roundhouse kick, and sent the masked guard crashing into the desk.

Breathing heavily, Karma hurried over to Ruby and helped her to her feet.

"Are you OK, honey?"

"I'm...I'm fine," Ruby replied, massaging the back of her head. "Those guards were tough. Did you see how that one guard communicated through the mask? I didn't know they could do that."

"That was strange, wasn't it?"

"Anyway, I can't believe this whole thing was a waste of time! That *bastard* sold us out! What are we going to do now?!"

A horrible gurgling noise came from behind them. The two women turned and the blood drained out of their faces. Benjamin was twitching on the floor – he was still alive. They ran over and knelt next to him.

"Hnk..Passw...passwo..." he mumbled, lines of blood pouring out of his mouth. Karma and Ruby grimaced at the red puddle pooling underneath him.

"Oh, Benjamin. I'm so sorry. I...I know that you didn't have a choice..." Karma said. Tears pooled in her eyes.

"Listen to me...the password..."

"What password?" Ruby asked.

"The password to...hnk...my computer..." Benjamin mumbled. "The password is...Warhola. Go to...to my apartment. Find a file called H Index."

"What's on the file?"

"Everything about...Project...Hominum. I've...been adding to…it…for the past few…months. Find Gus...tav and…bring him…down. And tell Amber and the kids that I'm so...sor..." Benjamin whispered. With one final gasp, he closed his eyes and died.

Karma covered her mouth and stifled a sob. Then, with a trembling hand, she reached over, closed Benjamin's eyes, and slowly stood up. Even Ruby, despite the betrayal that she had just gone through, felt a wave of sadness roll through her at the sight of the dead man.

"Let's go find that index," Karma whispered mournfully, and the two women left the bowling alley.

CHAPTER TWELVE

"Ugh. Why did I choose to wear these muttonchops?" Brody asked, scratching the sides of his face.

Cole, Gabe, and Brody were standing inside an oval-shaped reception room. Cole was clad in a brown regency tailcoat with white pants, Brody wore a light green waistcoat with cream breeches and a vest, and Gabe was dressed in grey pants and a black top hat with a black jacket; their teeth chattered due to a cold draft that was hanging in the air. They all had fake moustaches and beards glued to their faces.

"What do you think this place is?" Gabe asked.

"I don't know," Cole replied. "But something about it feels vaguely familiar." He wrapped his coat tighter around him and took in their elegant surroundings: metal sconces that held thin, white candles; a marble fireplace with a mirror above the mantle; framed oil paintings; polished mahogany furniture. Light poured in from a row of tall, curtained windows.

"You know, it'd be so much easier if *The Astrolabe* would drop us off *outside*. Getting stuck inside buildings is so annoying," Brody complained.

"I know. Come on, let's get out of this room and get our bearings straight," Cole replied.

They slowly opened a wooden door and peered outside. A long, carpeted hallway ran from left to right, and four marble pillars stood guard, separating the hallway from an entrance hall. A small crowd of people wearing either voluminous dresses or top hats moved through the entrance hall, pointing out paintings and observing the space.

"Maybe we're in a mansion?" Gabe suggested.

On their left, Cole noticed a regal dining room with patterned wallpaper and a large mahogany table. An elderly man with white hair and a hooked nose appeared in the doorway, scowled, and shut the door.

The three boys waited for the carpeted hallway to become clear, and then they tiptoed over to the marble pillars and hid behind them. The building they were in looked like a mix between an office building, a museum, and a royal palace.

"Look, that should lead us outside," Brody whispered, pointing to a pair of double doors straight ahead.

To the right of the double doors, a guard with a musket moved down a short set of carpeted stairs that led up to the second floor. As soon as the guard had left the room, Cole slipped into the crowd of onlookers, Brody and Gabe following close behind. The boys moved carefully through the crowd, trying their best to look like they belonged.

I really feel like I've seen this place before, Cole thought.

Luckily, none of the guests inside the stately mansion bothered them. Moving straight ahead, the boys passed underneath a glittering chandelier, went through the pair of double doors, and exited the building.

"Oh, *of course!* This isn't someone's mansion. This is the White House!" Gabe cried as they stepped outside.

Cole was shocked at how unglamorous the exterior looked. It seemed rather plain, just an imperious manor house that could probably hold a large family of ten. His eyes passed over the ornamental pediment that rested above a pair of twin pillars, the all-white exterior of the building, and the thin windows with wooden shutters. In 1835, it just seemed like a large mansion, not the epicenter of power in America.

Miles of empty land stretched out on every side of the White House, and it was muddy, overgrown, and undeveloped. Bare trees, like skeletal hands, reached out of the cold earth and tried to grasp the turbulent gray sky. It was the middle of winter, and the air was crisp and freezing. Cole felt a sense of unreality -- there were no power lines or lamp posts anywhere. It was like he was standing on the set of a period film, but this was real. He turned his head and noticed several men working the fields that spread out in front of the White House.

"So, we know that Andrew Jackson gets assassinated at the U.S. Capitol in about two hours," Gabe said. He took out his cell phone and pulled up a picture. "I took a photo of this before we left. It's a map from the 1860's, but it should still be relatively accurate. Hmm let's see...the Capitol building should be northwest of here." He shrank the picture, pulled up a compass, and held it out in front of him. "This way! Follow me."

Unfortunately, the driveway that ran in front of the White House was devoid of any carriages or horses, so the boys were forced to make their journey on foot. For the next forty minutes, they trekked across a wide stretch of soggy and frozen grass, past thick clusters of sequoia and pine trees, in the direction of the U.S. Capitol. At one point, Brody gasped as his boot sank into a puddle of mud.

"I wonder how Dad and Sabina are doing," Cole mused as they walked. "Your parents, too,

Gabe. Not to mention Ruby and Karma. I hope they're safe. I'm starting to get worried."

"Ruby and Karma have been through a lot, but they're tough. I know they can handle themselves," Gabe answered. "Man, I can't even explain to you how strange it is seeing my mom and dad together. Until this mess of a situation, they couldn't even be in the same room without fighting! I wouldn't be surprised if they've already gotten into a screaming match..."

"Aloicius told us that they'll be taken care of...but I don't know. Anything could be happening..." Cole said. His stomach twisted painfully with dread.

"Aloicius wouldn't *dare* let anything bad happen to them," Brody said.

"Why do you say that?"

"It just makes sense! If we find out that he, say, allowed them to be hurt, then we'd (obviously) refuse to complete this mission and the Master Timeline would be screwed," Brody answered matter-of-factly. "So, for that reason, Aloicius would never let anything bad happen to them."

Cole and Gabe weren't convinced, but they decided to remain quiet.

They eventually came upon a wide dirt road that led towards a cluster of wooden buildings rising up in the distance.

"This road should lead us to the Capitol building. Come on -- let's stay focused and get this done. We're almost finished," Gabe said.

"You're right, we *are* almost finished," Brody said as they made their way down the road. "And thank God for that. You know, I'll admit that, over the past few years, ever since I started traveling through time, I've seen some incredible things. I've gotten to travel the world, meet fantastic people from history, and now I can even say that I've seen *flying saucers!* That never would've happened without *The Astrolabe.* But...between the burden of knowing the fates of historical people that we encounter and having to constantly fix everything...time travel is just too much. So, after we get back home, Arthur has to shut down *The Astrolabe* once and for all."

"I agree. After everything that has happened? It only makes sense," Cole said.

The boys were quiet for several minutes as they continued walking down the road. Cole shivered in the cold rain and pulled his coat closer around him. A group of men on horseback slowly passed by them.

"I still can't believe we're actually here to save Andrew Jackson, that disgusting racist," Brody said.

"Is that true?" Gabe asked. "I'll be honest, I didn't really pay attention in history class."

"Oh yeah, he was *awful*," Brody answered. "Like, probably a sociopath. His terrible economic policies led to a recession that lasted for seven years. And, if that wasn't bad enough, his administration removed and killed thousands of Native Americans and he committed war crimes during the Seminole War! The man is a monster, and we shouldn't be rescuing him...but, alas, here we are. Obviously, I don't advocate violence, but it's no surprise that the first recorded physical attack *and* the first assassination attempt against a U.S. President were both directed at Andrew Jackson."

Moments later, the dirt road led them through the collection of wooden buildings. They walked by squat, shack-like houses that stood next to lopsided brick shops with bold advertisements painted across their walls. The boys were shocked to see a cow wandering the streets.

"There it is!" Cole said, pointing at a domed white structure in the distance. The state of the U.S. Capitol Building was shocking -- the dome at the center of it was open and half-finished, surrounded by cranes and wooden scaffolding.

"But...this doesn't make any sense. We shouldn't be seeing it like this at this point in time," Brody said.

"I guess this must be another result of the disturbances in the Master Timeline," Gabe answered.

As they got closer to the Capitol Building, they passed by a morose family of four, draped in filthy rags, who were selling wilted vegetables in the street. They shivered and their breath hung in the air. Cole felt awful for them. This was a difficult world to live in, a hardscrabble existence where you needed to be tough to survive.

More human misery greeted Cole, Brody, and Gabe as they continued walking through the town. Drunk and filthy people wandered the streets aimlessly or urinated against storefronts. There was a stink in the air, a mixture between animal manure and swamp gas.

As they turned a corner and strode past a dry goods store, a modest town square appeared. Wooden storefronts surrounded a large stone well, and a group of wealthy women wearing silk bonnets and long dresses with poofy sleeves walked by. Not a single mechanical could be seen anywhere.

"DAMN YOU!" a voice suddenly shouted.

The group of women abruptly stopped in their tracks and turned their heads in the direction of panicked cries that were coming from off in the distance.

"What was that?" Brody asked. "Should we go and see?"

"I don't know...we should probably focus on the mission," Cole answered.

"It will only take a second! Come on, let's go!" Brody said.

Cole and Gabe followed him as he ran towards the source of the noise.

They eventually stumbled upon a crowd that was gawking at an angry, grey-haired white man wearing tan breeches and a white Regency shirt. He was standing over an elderly black man who was groveling on the ground.

"What have I told you?!" the grey-haired man bellowed. He leaned back and slammed his boot into the black man's back. The black man screamed in pain and writhed on the ground, digging his hands into the mud.

"Why isn't anyone doing anything?" Gabe whispered.

Cole looked around and his heart went cold – the crowd was staring at the violence with passive expressions on their faces, as if they were watching a television program.

Something inside him snapped.

"STOP IT! What the hell are you doing?!" he yelled. Without thinking, he shoved the grey-haired man to the cold ground.

"How...How *dare* you!" the grey-haired man growled as he scrambled to his feet. "This is my property, and I will do whatever I want with him!"

"*Property?*" Cole roared. He lunged for the grey-haired man again, but Brody and Gabe held him back.

"Please stop, sir. I don't want any trouble," the elderly black man said. He was trembling and was covered in mud. "I-I dropped my master's package. It was my fault."

"That's right, Abraham. You don't want any trouble, right? Now. You better listen..." The grey-haired man approached Cole and puffed his chest out, rising to his full height. "If I ever see you around here again, I will alert the constable. You are not wanted here."

Cole glared at the aggressive man, stunned and disgusted, but didn't say anything. Then, the grey-haired man grabbed Abraham by the arm and dragged him away.

"Are you OK?" Brody asked Cole.

"I'm...I'm fine," Cole replied. "I'm sorry, I don't know what came over me."

"It's difficult not interfering in the flow of time, isn't it?" Brody said.

The small crowd surrounding the boys stared at them, looks of anger and judgement on their faces.

"What are you looking at?!" Cole yelled at the crowd. "Yeah, you're right, Brody. Time travel really messes with your emotions. Let's get out of here."

Feeling rattled by the violence that they had just witnessed, the three boys turned and continued walking towards the U.S. Capitol building.

CHAPTER THIRTEEN

The U.S. Capitol building appeared up ahead, hallowed and imposing. The awe-inspiring white stone temple had similar characteristics to the White House; rectangular wings running left and right and thin windows dotting the exterior. A long flight of stairs led up to a portico and colonnade that guarded a pair of front doors.

"What time is it?" Cole asked.

Gabe looked at his watch and said, "Wow, we got here in great time! According to the revised Master Timeline, Andrew Jackson will be assassinated within the next ten minutes. Richard Lawrence has to be around here somewhere."

"Can we go over our plan again?" Cole asked.

"Using the Invisibility Vambrace, I'll sneak up on Richard and subdue him before he shoots Andrew Jackson," Gabe explained. "Cole, you'll hide nearby and follow him with your blaster, just in case anything goes wrong. And Brody? You can just, um, watch what happens."

Through a thick cluster of oak trees, a handsome man suddenly appeared and started walking quickly down the dirt road. A dark mustache clung to his upper lip, and he was dressed in expensive clothing -- a long wool frock coat, tan trousers, and a top hat.

"Wait a minute. That's him!" Brody whispered excitedly.

The stranger looked just like any other wealthy businessman walking down the street, but, upon closer inspection, signs of dysfunction were visible: scuff marks on the ends of his boots; wear and tear at the elbows of his frock coat; grease stains on his trousers.

Richard Lawrence mumbled to himself and laughed strangely while he walked. "One does *not* treat *Richard the Third* in this fashion! Why is Jackson keeping my money? I WANT IT BACK!"

"Poor man. He seems very troubled," Gabe whispered.

"Oh, he definitely is," Brody replied. "Some historians think that the paint fumes he inhaled while he worked as a house painter contributed to his mental decline."

"Come on, let's follow him. He'll lead us to Andrew Jackson," Cole said. "But stay alert! This man is dangerous."

The boys followed Richard closely as he made his way toward the East Portico of the U.S. Capitol building. He moved quickly down the road with a threatening gait.

"Can you hand me the Invisibility Vambrace?" Gabe whispered to Cole.

"Actually...do you mind if I do it?" Brody asked.

Cole looked at him in confusion. "A-Are you sure? You don't have --"

"Hey, I'm not going to let you two have all the glory!" Brody joked.

Cole smiled warmly and handed him the Invisibility Vambrace. It folded around his wrist and he disappeared.

The boys moved out of the way of an oncoming horse-drawn carriage, hurried over to the set of wide stone stairs, and hid out of sight. They were shocked to see that there was no security patrolling the doors into the East Portico.

Richard moved quickly up the flight of stairs, his left hand stuffed into his coat pocket, and hid behind a tall white pillar. Gabe and Cole pointed their blasters at him while Brody raced up the stairs.

Suddenly, Andrew Jackson burst through the set of doors that led into the East Portico. The U.S. President was surrounded by a group of imperious men in long black cloaks and dark top hats. He looked grizzled and angry. A disagreeable expression rested on his sallow face, and thick tufts of unruly white hair protruded out of his large head.

Richard gripped his pistol tightly and waited for Andrew Jackson to get close to him. Any second now, a gunshot would go off.

Come on, Brody, move faster! he screamed in his mind as he ran towards Richard. He was nearly there...

When Brody was mere feet from him, Richard suddenly aimed at Andrew Jackson and fired -- a strangely muffled *bang* rang out. Brody skidded to a halt. Was he too late?

"Blast it!" Richard mumbled. Miraculously, the bullet had lodged itself into the barrel and jammed the pistol. It had failed!

Just as the assassin reached into his pocket and pulled out a second pistol, ready to fire, Brody bounded forward and slammed into him, knocking him roughly to the ground. With another loud *bang,* the second gun went off.

"*BRODY!*" Cole screamed. His heart pounding painfully in his chest, he and Gabe lowered their blasters and ran up the flight of stairs.

This time, a bullet had successfully fired, but it had flown over Andrew Jackson's head and lodged itself into a wall of the U.S. Capitol building. Small chunks of stone crumbled and fell around the edges of the bullet hole.

"You…You *scoundrel!*" Andrew Jackson cried, and Brody jumped out of the way as the cantankerous old man began to strike Richard over and over again with his cane. "You weak and pathetic *fool!* How *dare* you try and shoot me! Who do you work for? Did John C. Calhoun put you up to this?"

Cole, Gabe, and Brody stared, frozen in horror, at the chaos unfolding in front of them. Richard screamed and cowered on the ground while he tried to deflect the harsh blows that were raining down on him. If the three boys didn't intervene soon, Andrew Jackson was going to beat him to death!

Luckily, no intervention was necessary. The next moment, a man with dark brown hair that was parted in the middle suddenly jumped into the fray and pulled Andrew Jackson away from Richard Lawrence.

"Unhand me, Davy Crockett!" Andrew Jackson shouted.

Davy Crockett? Cole thought in surprise.

The failed assassin was dragged to his feet. A trickle of blood ran down his face from a cut on his forehead. He thrashed about wildly.

"Do you know whom you are manhandling? I'm Richard the Third! This man must fall in order for me to rise!" he bellowed, pointing an accusatory finger at Andrew Jackson.

A bright flash of light suddenly exploded above the city, nearly blinding everyone who was outside at that moment, and by the time that it died down, the sky had returned to normal.

Davy Crockett said to the boys, "Thank you for your help, gentleman. You saved the president! Is there anything that we can do –"

"They didn't save me!" Andrew Jackson snarled as he furiously wiped dirt off his coat. "I had everything under control!"

Davy Crockett looked at the boys sheepishly and muttered, "Well...thank you for your help, anyway."

Andrew Jackson, Davy Crockett, and the group of men in black cloaks dragged Richard away.

"Yes! We did it! But...what happens to Richard Lawrence now?" Gabe asked.

"Well, he was sent to live in various asylums for the rest of his life," Brody answered. "Unfortunately, Andrew Jackson gained an even bigger reputation. His supporters thought that God protected him from the assassination attempt. Just what he needed – another boost to his ridiculous ego."

As the boys made their way back to the White House, moving slowly due to the heavy feeling of exhaustion that had suddenly settled on them, they passed through the small cluster of buildings again. Cole massaged his aching back. At that moment, the only thing that he wanted was to get back onto the warm train, rest his tired feet, and get to the next location as quickly as possible. Unfortunately, that wasn't possible yet -- there was still work to be done. They had almost completed the mission. Victory was so close!

"OK, boys. The final item on our list is going to be the most difficult one," Gabe said. "But first, I've got to thank you, Brody. The way you tackled Richard to the ground? That was pretty amazing." He moved over to Brody and patted him good-naturedly on the back.

"Oh! Well…d-don't mention it," Brody replied with a smile. He blushed deeply.

"So, the last thing we have to do is somehow locate a lost Samuel Adams and, presumably, return him to colonial Boston. The biggest problem, though, is that we have no idea where he is, and the history books on *The Astrolabe* had no information."

"Didn't you say that he was last seen around here during this time period?" Cole asked.

"Yeah, but I read that on a conspiracy theory blog. What are the odds of that actually being true?"

"Yeah, you're probably right, it's not very likely. But why don't we walk around for a bit and shout out his name or something?" Cole suggested.

Gabe closed his eyes and thought for a moment.

"Hey...that's not a bad idea. It's a place to start, at the very least. If it doesn't work, we can always try to come up with something else."

For the next hour, the boys walked down the muddy streets of Washington, D.C. and called out for Samuel Adams, cupping their hands around their mouths to project their voices.

"SAMUELLLLLLL!"

"SAMUEL ADAMS, ARE YOU THERE?"

However, a sudden downpour of icy rain, along with deafening silence, was the only response that they received. Men and women who saw them on the streets turned away from them and fled. Cole, Brody, and Gabe glowered with frustration but continued their search.

As they walked past a large red brick church that was on the outskirts of the cluster of buildings, they suddenly came upon a middle-aged man who was banging loudly on the front doors. He had a pale and doughy face, expressive eyebrows, not much of a chin, and a short gray wig perched on top of his head. His clothes were streaked with dirt and mud, and he had a wild and panicked expression on his pale face.

"Allow me entrance, I beg of you!" he cried as he pounded the doors with his fists. "I am in need of assistance. Please!"

Across from the church, a small group of concerned townspeople stood on the side of the muddy road and stared at him curiously.

"MR. ADAMSSSS? ARE YOU THERE?" Brody shouted.

The desperate man in the powdered wig stopped what he was doing and turned to stare at the three boys, his eyes bulging in panic. "Wh-Who is that who calls for me?!"

Strangely, he was only wearing a tricorn hat, a thin white shirt, and colonial breeches over white stockings, and his body was shivering violently from the cold.

"Did...Did he just say...?" Gabe whispered excitedly.

"HEY, YOU! Is your name Samuel Adams?" Brody shouted at the stranger.

"How do you know that?" the man replied, his brow furrowing in confusion.

The inside of Cole's chest felt like it was popping with warm fireworks, and his eyes lit up with excitement. He couldn't believe their luck!

"Mr. Adams, we've been looking for you. You have to come with us right now! It's very important."

Samuel's brow furrowed. "You must be mad to think that I will agree to that. I will not be going anywhere with you, for you are strangers to me.

135

However, I am in need of assistance. I don't know where I am, and –"

"Come with us. *Right now!*" Cole barked. He pointed his blaster at him, suddenly changing tactics. He was eager to get to Boston now, and he didn't have time to play nice.

"Stay back!" Samuel Adams said. He turned around and ran away in the opposite direction.

"Come back! We can help you!" Brody shouted.

"Dammit! I'm getting so tired of chasing after people," Cole groaned.

Gathering what remained of their strength, the boys ran after him, making their way past a tavern and a line of wooden stables, before Samuel abruptly took a hard right and left the town, leading them into a thicket of trees.

"Leave me be!" he yelled hoarsely.

Cole, in the lead, pushed and shoved past rough and emaciated tree branches that scraped his face as he tried to grab Samuel. One thing was for sure -- he was going to take this man back to colonial Boston no matter what.

Samuel pressed on, but it was obvious that he was starting to get winded. He took ragged, gasping breaths, stumbling over the snowy underbrush. Navigating this frozen forest, with its gnarled and icy trees, was quickly proving to be a herculean task.

"Samuel!" Brody suddenly cried out. The three boys watched as, with a low groan, the middle-aged man in colonial dress caught his leather shoe on the edge of a tree stump, tripped over his feet, and landed in a pile of snow.

Cole, Brody, and Gabe stopped running and slowly approached Samuel's limp body. The unconscious man was now completely bald. His wig lay on the ground next to him.

"I can't believe it – we actually found him!" Brody said.

Gabe and Cole grabbed Samuel's arms and legs and they carried him back to *The Astrolabe.*

CHAPTER FOURTEEN

Back at Atmos, Arthur and Sabina were sitting on the cold, wet floor of their jail cell, resting their backs against a rough stone wall. It was quiet, except for the steady *drip drip drip* of water droplets that came from a corner of the room. Arthur had his pocket watch opened in his lap and, using a screwdriver and a pair of needle nose pliers, he passed the long hours of their captivity by tinkering with its complicated interior. An interesting idea was starting to form at the back of his mind, but he dared not say it out loud just yet.

With a low groan, he raised his arms into the air and stretched out his sore back. Then, he leaned over and scratched at his cast; his injured leg was itching like crazy.

"Honey, try not to scratch it," Sabina said listlessly. She felt weary and lethargic. "It will only make it worse."

Arthur sighed. Dark circles hung under his eyes. "How long have we been in here?"

Sabina turned her head and consulted a long line of tally marks that she had been carving into the wall. "We're at sixty-one hours...but time moves strangely here, so I don't even really know how accurate this is."

Arthur sighed again. He leaned back against the wall and resumed poking at the pocket watch.

"What are you doing with that thing, anyway?" Javier asked. He was sitting in a shadowy corner of the jail cell.

"I'm just, um, working on something. An idea. My watch could prove to be helpful to us," Arthur answered. He groaned, moved his leg, and shifted uncomfortably on the floor.

"You think a *watch* is going to help us?" Javier asked, rolling his eyes. "Unbelievable..."

Arthur ignored him and turned to Sabina. "Do you think the kids are OK?"

"Oh, I'm sure that they're fine. Don't worry. Cole, Ruby, and their friends are doing everything they can to set things right."

"I thought that they *at least* would've been done by *now*..." Lucia grumbled. She stared into space with her eyes half open.

"We just have to stay hopeful. They'll be back soon!" Sabina insisted. She tried her best to project an air of confidence, but it was difficult because she felt so hungry and weak.

Several minutes of strained silence passed.

"You know something? You always stay positive in any situation," Arthur said. "I don't know how you do it. I love that about you."

"Well, I try. After going through everything that I went through with my ex-husbands, I've realized that falling into despair doesn't help me solve my problems. It's not always easy to remember that, though," she said.

"Not to mention that you're incredibly smart. I love the way your mind works."

Sabina smiled and blushed. "You're sweet."

A faint smile clung to Arthur's lips. "You know, darling...I was thinking..."

"Yes?"

"Well...I've wanted to ask you this for a while..." He paused and took a deep breath.

"Honey, what is it?"

"I know that we haven't been dating for a long time. But, listen -- I'm not getting any younger. And, after everything that we've been through together...things have become clearer for me."

Despite her fatigue, Sabina sat up straighter. "Arthur, are you...are you asking me what I think you're asking me?"

"I don't have a proper ring with me, but...will this do?" Arthur yanked a piece of gold wire off his pocket watch and bent it into the shape of a ring. "Will you marry me?"

Tears ran down Sabina's cheeks and her face lit up with joy.

"*Of course* I'll marry you, my sweet old man!"

"Hey!" Arthur chuckled. He slipped the makeshift ring onto her finger – it fit perfectly.

"This is wonderful! But...are you sure?"

"Absolutely. No matter what the situation is, I want you to be with me. I love you." Arthur pulled her in for a deep kiss.

"Congratulations," Javier said. He clapped weakly.

"Yeah...congratulations," Lucia mumbled. She groaned and put her hands on her stomach. "Normally, I would bake something to celebrate. What I wouldn't give for some machaca right now. I would *kill someone* for machaca in a thick burrito...green bell peppers...warm baked beans on the side. *Oh, for God's sake!* It's been almost three days without food and water! How much longer can we do this?"

"Way to ruin the moment, Lucia," Javier grumbled.

"Shut up, Javier!"

"You've been complaining non-stop since we were put in this cell!"

"That's not true!"

"You only think of yourself. This is just one of the many reasons why we divor --"

"*Enough!*" Sabina yelled loudly. The squabbling ex-couple fell silent and looked at her.

"Your arguing is wasted energy! It accomplishes nothing. All of us are hungry and thirsty. All of us are tired. Enough already!"

"I've got to get out of here!" Lucia yelled. She got to her feet, a frenzied look on her face. "We have to do something! If we don't, we're all going to die!"

"Don't be ridiculous," Javier said, rolling his eyes. "Die? We just have to wait for Gabe, Cole, and Brody to come back! They're going to save us. Besides, we can't upset Aloicius."

"I don't care about Aloicius! Or Thelonia! Do you think I trust them? *Hell no!* Where is the food that we were promised? And the medical attention?"

"Honestly? She's right," Arthur admitted.

"What?" Javier cried, his eyebrows raising in alarm.

Arthur slowly got to his feet. He wasn't sure if it was the effect from his impromptu marriage proposal or something else, but a sudden rush of energy was pulsing through him.

"This has taken much, much longer than we expected, and we're not getting food and water. We have to act."

"*Thank you!* Thelonia has *definitely* been lying to us. I can't stand her smug face," Lucia said passionately. "We have to sneak out of here. At the very least, we can find some food. Maybe even an exit! But I can't stay in here and waste away any longer."

"While we were getting taken here, I saw someone open a large gold door and enter a huge restaurant. Or maybe it was a kitchen? Anyway, there should be plenty of food and water in there," Arthur said.

"Wait a minute! Those glowing beings are clearly very powerful. What if they catch us and punish us?" Javier asked.

"Our situation has become dire. We have to try," Lucia insisted. "We'll just have to hope that they don't catch us. Who is with me?" She looked at them, fire burning in her eyes.

"But there's no way out of here!"

"Actually…that's not entirely true. I think I can help with that, but I just need some more time to get this pocket watch working," Arthur said.

"What do you mean?" Lucia asked.

"Give me complete silence for a few hours and I *might* be able to produce something."

"Hmm...OK. Go for it," Javier said.

Arthur pulled a tiny blowtorch out of his jacket pocket, put the pocket watch on the ground, and set to work.

For the next two hours, everyone stared at him anxiously while he worked. Bright orange sparks popped under Arthur's hands, and small metal pieces of the pocket watch littered the floor. Sweat from his exertion ran down his forehead, and he dabbed at it with a towel.

"So. Um...I'm not trying to rush you or anything, but...any luck yet?" Javier asked.

Arthur was hunched over, working feverishly, his fingers moving across the timepiece. "I'm-I'm having trouble connecting the *stupid* Shearer cable to the X-3 bolt, which is supposed to send an electrical charge to – UGH! DAMMIT!" he yelled in frustration, and he slammed the pocket watch onto the ground.

"What's wrong?" Sabina asked.

"The damn thing won't work! It's –"

A red laser abruptly shot out of the center of the time piece, and the blast struck the opposite wall and bored a tiny hole into it.

"H-How did you do that?!" Javier cried.

Arthur scrambled to his feet and cheered. "HA! I *knew* that I could get it to work! *Oof...*" He winced, grabbed his injured leg, and sank to the ground. Sabina hurried over and put her arm around his shoulders.

"Aim that laser at the cell bars and knock them down!" Lucia cried.

"Wait, we don't know if our captors will come back. It's best if we keep our escape as secret as possible," Sabina said. "Here, Javier. Why don't you take the watch and aim it at the ground underneath the bars? That way, you can crawl out of this cell, instead of smashing right through."

"Press the center of the watch and it will fire," Arthur said faintly, gritting his teeth in pain. A burning sensation was running up his injured leg.

Javier aimed and fired. The laser struck the ground and immediately began to carve out a large hole. The floor sizzled and popped and smoked. When the hole was big enough for a human to crawl through, he stopped.

"Come on! Everybody through!" Lucia said.

"I...I can't," Arthur said mournfully. "My leg, remember?"

"Oh...right. What should we do? We can't just leave you."

"I'll stay with him," Sabina said. She grabbed his hand.

"Are you sure?"

"Yes, but you two go ahead! We'll wait here."

Lucia crawled through the tunnel and emerged on the other side of the jail cell. Javier followed her.

"We'll find food and water and come back for you!" he said.

"Please hurry," Sabina urged.

Lucia and Javier turned and walked up a long stone staircase before stepping out of an arched wooden door. They found themselves in one of the mirrored halls that seemed to go on for miles.

"Do you recognize any of this?" Javier asked.

"Hmm...not at all. Let's, um, go to the left? See where we end up. We can always backtrack."

Their surroundings were eerily quiet. The only sound that could be heard was the clicking of Lucia's boots on the floor as they made their way down numerous hallways, all of which looked nearly identical.

"So...it's nice to see you again," Lucia said after they had been walking for a few minutes. "You look, um, healthy."

"Oh. Well...thanks. I've been trying to go to the gym more," Javier said uncomfortably. "You look great yourself. How is Dallas? Do you like it?"

"I do! It's much warmer than Mechanica City, but it's nice. I have a great new job. I've met someone. Everything is great. What about you?"

"I'm glad you're happy. And I don't love the weather in Boston but I'm making more money, so that has been nice," Javier responded.

There was a moment of awkward silence.

"Well...Cole seems like a nice boy. I'm glad that Gabriel has found someone," Lucia said.

"Yeah, he seems like a good kid. His father, though? A total nutjob," Javier replied.

They turned a corner and came upon yet another mirrored hallway. Dozens of their reflections stared back at them.

"Are we going the right way?"

"Um…I don't know anymore. Everything looks the same. Should we go back?" Lucia said.

Strange and muffled noises came from behind a solid gold door that stood on their left, further down the hall. A glowing light peeked out from beneath the door.

"Wait, a gold door! Maybe that's the restaurant that Arthur told us about!" Javier said.

Javier and Lucia cautiously approached the door. They could hear strange popping and grinding sounds.

Javier held a finger to his lips. Lucia nodded and slowly pushed the door open.

On the other side of the door, a member of the Uhrzeit was standing in front of a flat black disc;

their back was to Lucia and Javier. In the corner of the room, an unconscious elderly man was laying on a metal examination table. Long wires protruded out of his body, snaked across the floor, and stuck into the Uhrzeit's arm.

The Uhrzeit member adjusted a few knobs on the black structure and stepped back. Then, they put a microphone to their mouth and said, "Testing. Testing. This is Aloicius, welcome to Atmos."

As they spoke, Aloicius's floating head materialized over the flat black disc and said the same words that the Uhrzeit member had just said. The man on the examination table groaned as the wires sticking out of him began to glow with a bright yellow light. This light moved through the wires and into the Uhrzeit member.

"What is this?!" Lucia cried.

The member of the Uhrzeit turned around and Lucia and Javier gasped – it was Thelonia! She stared at them with an irritated expression on her face.

"You two aren't supposed to be here," she said. She snapped her fingers and the floor beneath Javier and Lucia began to ripple and liquify, pulling them under like quicksand.

"Wh-What are you doing?!" Javier cried.

Within seconds, Javier and Lucia sank through the floor and landed back inside the jail cell.

CHAPTER FIFTEEN

The twelve-story Cheswick Hotel rose up in front of them. A dark and dilapidated building, the red-brick hotel took up an entire city block. There were wrought iron balconies in front of the horizontal rows of windows, and a neon sign that stuck out from the exterior that said, "Hotel Cheswick."

Ruby and Karma felt like frightened animals as they nervously approached the building. The hotel had an exciting, yet formidable, presence -- most of the windows were either blacked out or smashed. The front entrance was blocked by heavy furniture.

"So...this is where Gustav has been hiding this whole time?" Ruby asked.

"Yes, according to the files that Benjamin led us to. I can't believe it – an entire database with details about every single member of Project Hominum," she said, holding up a USB drive. "*Everything* is different now."

"I'm sorry that he died," Ruby said softly.

"Me too," Karma responded. She sniffled and wiped her eyes. "And I'm sorry that you had to see him like that. I promise you, he didn't want to betray us."

The two women silently stared up at the hotel for several minutes.

"Benjamin loved this hotel," Karma said mournfully. "Have you ever stayed here before?"

"No, I've never been here."

"It has so much fascinating history. It was built in 1885 and catered to unique and creative customers. Many famous artists have stayed here!"

"Really? Wow, I've never even heard of this place! How do we get inside?" Ruby whispered.

"Follow me," Karma said, and they walked over to the right side of the hotel. Down a flight of steps, a door rested at the bottom – a side entrance.

"Anything could be waiting for us inside, so we have to stay focused and be very careful," she said. "Ask Gustav your questions as quickly as possible so that I can...you know...take care of things."

Ruby nodded and held her blaster in her hands -- she was ready. They descended the steps down to the side entrance.

The door ended up being unlocked, so they let themselves inside. A dark entrance lobby greeted them. Shadows crawled up walls that were covered with eclectic and colorful paintings, and avant-garde sculptures either hung from the ceiling or stood in corners. Ruby and Karma slowly walked by a multicolored fireplace.

Near the back of the entrance lobby was a door that led to the main staircase. A front desk had been placed next to the door, and it was chipped in several places and covered in a thick layer of dust. A deep crack ran up a wall that was next to it – it was clear that the chaos from the streets of Mechanica City had found its way inside the hotel.

Ruby jumped at a creaking sound that came from above them.

"What was that?" she whispered.

"I don't know. All of the tenants have vacated the premises, so it's probably him," Karma replied. "Follow me and stay quiet."

They passed by the front desk, walked through the door, and craned their necks to look at a cast iron staircase that spiraled upwards into darkness. A single emergency light on the wall was the only light source in the stairwell, and it cast eerie shadows across the walls.

Something moved above them.

151

"There's the sound again!" Karma whispered.

As they slowly and quietly made their way up the cast iron steps, guns at the ready, they passed by more artwork. Canvases covered in bright paint sat on the walls next to framed black and white photographs of flowers.

They approached the first landing, and the stairwell around them was silent as a tomb. Straight ahead, they could see several square doors leading off a long, dark hallway. Ruby's heart began to pound furiously in her chest.

From behind a corner, the creaking sound came yet again. Ruby and Karma tensed, the hair on the back of their necks standing up. They slowly approached the corner.

Karma brought her phone up to her lips and said, "Gustav? Is that you?" An app deepened her voice to sound more like Benjamin.

There was a crashing sound and then a gold cat abruptly ran into view. Ruby and Karma screamed. The cat hissed and scampered past them.

"Oh my *GOD!*" Karma cried, putting her hand to her chest. "I feel like I almost had a heart attack, and I don't even have a heart!"

"That was ridi --"

Suddenly, one of the hotel room doors burst open and an elderly man sitting in a gold and silver wheelchair rolled out. He was holding three large bottles of vodka in his wrinkled arms.

"John, what the hell are you do – oh! Who are you?"

Ruby and Karma spun around and aimed their blasters at him. As soon as her eyes fell onto the old man, terrible memories flooded Ruby's mind and she was filled with rage.

Gustav threw his hands into the air and dropped the liquor bottles. One of them shattered on the ground.

"Remember me, you ugly bastard?" Ruby yelled. She pulled the trigger and an energy blast ripped through Gustav's shoulder. The old man screamed and his wheelchair rolled back and slammed against the wall. He slid out of his chair and fell to the floor, groaning in pain.

"Who…Who are you?" he said through gritted teeth. His shoulder spewed blood, and he covered it with a gnarled hand.

Ruby dragged him to his feet by the front of his shirt and slammed him against the wall. "Really? You don't remember me? That's probably because I was just a body to you, you bastard!"

Gustav's eyes stared into hers, and, after a moment, a look of realization passed across his face. "Ah! I remember you now. Jaxon's little toy." He barked out a raspy laugh.

"I'M NOT A TOY!" Ruby screamed in his face.

Gustav turned his head and glared at Karma. "I certainly know who *you* are, filthy robot."

"You're disgusting," Karma said.

Ruby shoved him against the wall again. "By the way, your friend Jaxon? He killed himself. He died like a trapped rat!"

Gustav smiled with bloody teeth and released an unhinged giggle that caused a chill to roll down Ruby's spine.

"Oh, I'm aware, sweetheart. I may be old, but I'm not senile. As soon as I learned that some of my Project Hominum brothers had watched him abruptly disappear…I knew that our glorious plan had been foiled."

"Ugh, you smell filthy," Ruby said, and she pushed Gustav away from her and he sank to the floor again. He looked terrible, even without his new shoulder injury: lanky, gray hair that fell past his ears, a scraggly beard, and bloodshot eyes. He looked like he hadn't slept in weeks.

Karma noticed that the hotel room behind Gustav was trashed with empty bottles and spoiled food on plastic trays. Piles of filthy clothes covered the stained floor. She grimaced and turned away.

"How long have you been living here?" she asked.

"Ever since Jaxon came back to Mechanica City with *her*," Gustav said, pointing a gnarled finger at Ruby. "I hid here so that no one could look for me and attempt to stop anything if they somehow discovered that I was involved with the movement." The sickly old man slowly crawled back into his wheelchair. He rolled over to the bottles of vodka, picked one up off the floor, took a long swig, and groaned in pain.

Ruby grimaced at the sight of him. This man, this horrendous bigot that had filled her thoughts with nightmares, now seemed so fragile and pathetic.

"So. I'm assuming that you've come to kill me, is that right?" Gustav asked, smirking.

"Would that really be so terrible? After everything that you've done? You deserve to be punished," Karma growled.

"Well...I guess I should've expected this. Throughout history, innocent men with revolutionary ideas have always been destroyed."

Ruby scoffed. "You have a *very* strange interpretation of the word 'revolutionary.'"

"But why do you need to punish me at all? You've won, haven't you? You saved the world and Project Hominum is basically gone. What else do you want?" Gustav asked. A phlegmy cough erupted out of him and he was doubled over for several seconds, hacking roughly.

155

"Won? We haven't won anything yet," Ruby barked. "Not a single one of your members has been punished for what has happened to Mechanica City! I want justice."

"Ah yes. 'Justice.' That elusive and disappointing concept."

Ruby ignored him. "Like I said, Jaxon is dead, so, now that I've got you in front of me, you're going to answer some questions."

Gustav smiled. "What do you want to know, sweetheart?"

"How did you learn about *The Astrolabe?* My father never told anyone about it."

"He didn't have to. I hate to break it to you, but your father is a very careless man. He left his blueprints just lying around on his desk. Anyone could have seen them."

"So, you're openly admitting that you're just a nosey rat who can't mind his own business," Karma said.

"You can judge me all you want, robot, but I would do it again. Everyone at Bennett Industries thought Arthur was such a genius, but I knew the truth. He was just a reckless, irresponsible fool who got by on his charm. Nothing more."

"I don't understand. Why did you target my father? What did he ever do to you?"

"Because *I hated that bastard!*" Gustav roared, slamming his fist onto the armrest of his wheelchair. "I could've had his job! I had designs in my head, too. But no, I was stuck in the patent office. You know, people liked me better than Arthur. They always said that he was eccentric behind his back. But he's privileged. Came from rich parents. How do you think he started Bennett Industries? Men like him are all the same."

"Liar! My grandparents were working class!" Ruby cried.

"Yeah yeah yeah. I know what I know, OK? He is garbage. He thought that he could fire me and get away with it? HA! I was ecstatic when he disappeared. But, alas, he came back. And then things got worse in Mechanica City."

"How did they get worse?" Karma asked.

"Robots are unnatural! And he let them all over his workplace. They take human jobs! Not only that, but they're disgusting to look at – they make me sick!" Gustav roared. As he became increasingly agitated, his face bloomed bright red.

"And then...UGH! *YOU!*" He pointed at Karma. "Karma's Act! That was the final straw. Mainstream media is lying – robots hate humans and want to replace us. Jaxon understood that. Many people in this city do, too. They know the downside to letting robots exist."

"None of that is true! How can you not see that? There is room for everyone," Ruby cried.

"Room for everyone?! *Robots use human blood for oil!* The government has been trying to keep it a secret for years! I've seen the evidence; I know what I'm talking about!"

There was a long and stunned silence. Karma leaned against the wall and pinched the bridge of her nose in frustration. The realization that this whole encounter was completely futile struck her forcefully, like a blow to the stomach. Gustav was sick, very sick, and would never be shown the error of his ways. He couldn't be reasoned with or helped.

"Nothing that you're saying makes any sense!" Ruby said. "You're *insane!* But you know what? I don't care. Everyone will learn that all this chaos was just a product of your twisted mind and nothing more. Most Mechanica City citizens don't hate mechanicals -- I know it! We can get things back to the way they used to be."

Gustav cackled again, took another long swig of vodka, and then sank into his chair. His face was sweaty and grey. "The way things used to be? Do you really think that it's going to be that simple? Everything will be perfect once I'm gone? Once every member of Project Hominum is put in jail? It's too late for that! You can't stop human nature."

"Hu...Human nature?" Karma whispered. Her face had gone slack and her shoulders slumped.

"Face it – Jaxon and I would never have been able to do what we did if we weren't able to organically attract people to our cause," Gustav explained. His breath came in ragged gasps. "Many people in this city wanted us to succeed. What are you going to do about them? Project Hominum is a nameless and faceless organization. You'll never be able to lock up all of them. How do you kill an idea?"

Ruby roared and punched the wall next to Gustav's face. "STOP IT! You're wrong! We won't allow any of your filthy ideas to gain traction in this city again!"

"Maybe...Maybe he has a point," Karma said mournfully.

"Karma!" Ruby cried.

"What? This old man's mind is obviously deranged...and yet, he has a point. How are we supposed to slow down what they've already started? What if we never could? I mean, there are thousands of names on that index."

"What index?" Gustav asked.

"Maybe there will *always* be people who hold negative views about mechanicals..." She leaned against the wall and put her face in her hands.

Ruby stood in place, rooted to the spot. She was devastated. Rage coursed through her body like an electric shock. This couldn't be how it ended.

"Then...Then I'll just kill you right here, you son of a bitch! This city may never go back to normal, but at least I'll have the satisfaction of seeing you dead!" She pressed her gun against his temple.

"Little rich girl," Gustav sneered. "You don't have the guts."

"SCREW YOU!" Ruby roared. She pressed the barrel of her gun harder against his temple, her hands shaking, tears running down her cheeks. Her finger hovered over the trigger.

Gustav glared at her, staring deeply into her eyes. Ruby shuddered – there wasn't any life behind his irises.

"Humans first!"

He bit down on something in his mouth and it made a crunching sound. White foam suddenly oozed out between his lips and his body started to seize. He gurgled and groaned in pain.

"NOOOOOOO!" Ruby screamed. She grabbed him by the front of his shirt and shook him roughly, but his head drooped to the side and his mouth fell open – he was dead.

"Well...it's over..." Karma said dejectedly.

Ruby lowered her blaster and shoved Gustav's lifeless body to the ground. She felt disgusted with everything.

"No...No, it's not! I won't accept that!"

"But Gustav got away. He wasn't punished at all."

"No, we can...we can still do this. Listen to me. I-I have an idea." She walked into Gustav's room and frantically started tearing it apart, overturning furniture and digging through drawers.

"What are you doing?!" Karma asked.

"Remember that signal that calls any Project Hominum member?"

"The one on their mask? Yes. Why?"

"Aha!" Ruby bent down and picked up a Project Hominum mask that was lodged behind a dresser. "Maybe...Maybe this isn't over yet! We can use this mask for, um, something. All we have to do is think of a new plan."

Karma shook her head. "No, Ruby. It's over for me."

"What are you talking about?" Ruby cried.

"I'm going back to help Cole."

"But...But why?"

"I can't do this anymore. Gustav is dead...Jaxon is dead...and, after everything that has happened, Project Hominum still exists. This has all been for nothing."

Ruby wiped away hot tears that had filled her eyes. "That's not true! We can't give up."

"It is true. We have to stop being naïve. Hatred for mechanicals will always exist."

"Well…what about me? What am I supposed to do now?"

Karma's bottom lip trembled. "Just stay here. I'll come back with the others when the mission is completed."

"Karma, wait!"

"I'm sorry, Ruby."

Karma turned and hurried out of the hotel, tears pouring down her face.

CHAPTER SIXTEEN

Inside a bedroom compartment on *The Astrolabe,* Gabe, Brody, Cole, and a mechanical woman named Mrs. Cunningham surrounded Samuel Adams. He was lying on a bed with an IV line sticking out of his arm. Mrs. Cunningham adjusted the IV bag and dabbed his forehead with a cold towel.

With a groan, he suddenly woke up and looked around at the group that surrounded his bed.

"He-Hello, Mr. Adams," Cole said softly. He didn't want to startle him.

Samuel Adams screamed, scrambled out of the bed, ripped out his IV, and backed away from them in a panic.

"Be careful!" Mrs. Cunningham cried.

Samuel pulled a knife out of his pocket and pointed it at them. "Wh-Where am I? Who are you?!"

"Calm down, sir! You're still weak," Brody said.

Samuel swayed where he stood before sitting down on the bed again. He slowly lowered his knife and looked around in a daze. "Please...don't hurt me."

"We're not going to hurt you!" Cole insisted. "We've brought you to *The Astrolabe* because you almost froze to death. How are you feeling?"

"Astrolabe? We...We are inside an astronomical instrument? How can that be?"

"No, that's just the name of the train that we're on."

Samuel Adams' face paled. "A train?!"

Cole and his companions looked at each other in confusion. Where to even start?

"Why don't you follow me?" Mrs. Cunningham asked. She smiled warmly and put a comforting hand on his shoulder. "I'm sure you're hungry. We can offer you food and provide an explanation about everything."

As they led Samuel down the hallways of the train, a blanket draped over his shoulders, he stared around at his surroundings with open-mouthed wonder. He was so stunned by the beauty of the locomotive that, child-like, he ran his hands over the compartment doors and touched the light fixtures.

"You said that this is...a *train?* What is a train?"

"Well, um, a train is basically a really long wagon that is made out of metal," Cole explained.

"Impossible," Samuel scoffed, but he continued looking around at everything in awe.

As soon as they had relaxed and settled into the front train compartment, Mrs. Cunningham handed Cole, his friends, and their Founding Father guest bowls of warm beef stew.

"So...can you tell us what you remember?" Brody asked.

"I will give my best effort. The experience was decidedly strange," Samuel replied. "I remember being in my home, preparing myself to leave for a meeting when, suddenly, a bright white flash of light erupted in the air and blinded me. When the light finally disappeared, I was somewhere else! I do not know how it happened. Nothing was recognizable to me. I wandered about for several hours...and then you approached me. God bless you! I apologize for running away from you. I was not thinking clearly."

"Oh, no apology necessary. We were happy to help," Cole said.

"Who are all of you? What am I doing here? And, please pardon my boldness, but...*what* are you?" Samuel asked, motioning to Mrs. Cunningham.

Cole's face flushed – how were they going to explain mechanicals?

"Um...well, this is Mrs. Cunningham. She's, um, wearing armor. She's our bodyguard that protects us."

"I'm wearing *what?*" Mrs. Cunningham said incredulously.

"Yes. *Armor,*" Brody insisted, flashing her a knowing look.

"Like a medieval knight?" Samuel asked.

"Exactly right. Like I said, she's our bodyguard. She, um, protects us and the train," Cole said.

"How queer," Samuel Adams said in awe.

"My name is Cole, and this is Brody, Gabe, and Mrs. Cunningham."

"It is nice to meet you. Now, what am I doing on this...this train? How does something like this exist?"

"Well...it's kind of a long story," Brody answered. "We are spies for the Sons of Liberty. We work in the colonies under Lord Dartmouth. We're inside a, um, secret new method of travel that the Sons of Liberty have been building."

"Is that so? Because I am quite sure that I have never seen any of you or this train before," Samuel said.

"Well...we tend to keep to ourselves. We're deep undercover," Brody replied. "Anyway, Lord Dartmouth sent soldiers to get rid of you. He, um, had you captured and abandoned in the middle of the Massachusetts wilderness. We discovered your location and rescued you."

Cole, once again, was blown away by Brody's ability to invent a compelling story.

"Lord Dartmouth? That *swine!* He thinks he can be rid of me? Well, as you have shown, my brothers in the Sons of Liberty will always protect me. We will never be defeated!" He smiled and hugged everyone in the room.

For the next hour, while everyone dug into their soup, Samuel Adams lowered his guard and slowly started to open up. As *The Astrolabe* made its way towards the 1770's Decade Station, he told them stories about his early life. He was born in Boston and grew up on Purchase Street, where his father, a respected church deacon, made and sold beer. His parents were devout Puritans, which was a major source of pride for him.

"They were quite strict when I was growing up, especially my father, but their values sustained me and guided me. Honesty, responsibility, and hard work served me well when I began my career. I would not be the man I am today without their teachings."

"They must be very proud of you," Gabe said.

"They have long since passed, but I can still feel them watching over me and protecting me."

When Cole asked him about his political career and his time with the Sons of Liberty, Samuel got an excited gleam in his eye and he began to talk very quickly, getting himself more and more worked up.

"And, as you know, we are *still* not represented in Parliament! Therefore, they can not levy taxes on us. It is *disgraceful!* We must break away from the Crown, and we *must do it now!*" He slammed his hand on the table.

Everyone jumped in surprise.

"My-My apologies. I am a passionate man and have been told on more than one occasion that I can be...somewhat overwhelming."

"Girl, same," Brody said.

"Anyway, when we return to Boston, I must get to the Old South Meeting House. An important meeting is being held there right now, one that I can not miss."

"What is the meeting about?" Brody asked, yawning widely. Now that he had finally eaten some food, he struggled to keep his eyes open and all he wanted to do was take a nap.

"But, as members of the Sons of Liberty, surely you must know! We will be discussing the plan."

"The plan?"

"You know…the plan concerning the dumping of the tea!" Samuel said, his thin lips curling into a mischievous smile.

"Oh. Right. Of course! *That* meeting!" Brody said. He kicked himself internally for his gaffe.

"We must do something dramatic. Paying even one small tax allows Parliament to set a precedent of taxation, and that is unacceptable. When one is dealing with trying times, always believe in yourself and never surrender. We can not give up on this."

Cole sat back in his chair and smiled, feeling deeply impressed by the spirited man that was sitting at the table with him. Samuel Adams was clearly someone who didn't allow self-doubt or fear to control him. He continued eating his stew, wishing that he could be more like him.

Suddenly, a loud crack of thunder rolled through the air and a bright light flashed outside the windows.

"What was that?" Cole asked nervously.

Everyone moved to the windows and pushed aside the curtains. Strange events were unfolding right outside of *The Astrolabe's* doors; thick blasts of white lightning flashed, striking the multicolored air that rushed by. Thunder boomed in the distance.

"Is that...weather?" Brody asked. "Can wormholes have weather?"

"I have no idea!" Cole said. He jumped in surprise as another bright streak of lightning flashed by the window.

"What is a wormhole?" Samuel asked.

"Umm...we'll explain later," Brody responded.

"Look at that!" Gabe cried.

Yet another bolt of lightning rained down and struck the multicolored air, but, this time, a smaller, separate wormhole opened. Inside this new wormhole, a turbulent scene was unfolding: a crowd of young men and women wearing shirts with psychedelic patterns, along with a handful of colorful drag queens, were yelling and throwing bricks at police officers outside of a New York City bar.

But, just as quickly as the smaller wormhole appeared, it closed and disappeared.

Another lightning bolt rained down and struck the top of *The Astrolabe*. With a grinding noise, the train lurched dangerously from side to side.

"What is that smell?" Cole asked nervously.

Everyone turned and looked at the control panel that was at the front of the compartment. Plumes of dark smoke were starting to pour out of it.

"*NO!*" Mrs. Cunningham screamed. She ran over to the control panel and started pressing buttons. A bright orange spark erupted underneath her fingers. "The lightning storm must have short-circuited it! *No no no!* The brakes aren't working!"

"What?!" Gabe yelled.

"We're approaching the 1770's Decade Station!"

Like a smoke bomb going off, panic filled the room. If they didn't do something soon, they would miss their train stop and (possibly) crash. Samuel Adams groaned and put his head in his hands.

Cole's forehead broke out in a nervous sweat, and he started to get tunnel vision. *This is no time for an anxiety attack!* he screamed in his head. He took several deep breaths, closed his eyes, and, with a great deal of effort, forced himself to focus. They could get through this...he hoped.

"Mrs. Cunningham, what can we do to fix this? There has to be something!" he said.

"Well...someone will have to, um, climb underneath the train and pull the large green lever," she said sheepishly. "It will send an emergency supply of power to the main control panel. I would

171

do it myself, but...I'm embarrassed to admit that I'm terrified of heights."

"I'll do it," Gabe said without hesitation.

A rush of anxiety burned in Cole's chest at this announcement. "Shouldn't we take some time to think about this?"

"I don't mind heights, and we don't have any time to waste. But I'll need some help to keep me safe. Mrs. Cunningham, do you have any rope that can secure me to the train?"

She nodded, hurried out of the room, and, moments later, returned with a long nylon rope. "Will this work?"

"That's perfect," Gabe replied.

"Wait, things are moving too fast. Are you sure about this?" Cole asked.

"Absolutely. I can do this," he insisted.

Mrs. Cunningham slipped the rope around Gabe's waist, tied a knot, and led him over to the exit. She slid the door open and a strong gust of wind blew inside, rifling everyone's hair and clothes. Cole looked down at the yawning chasm below and his stomach did an anxious flip.

Gabe took a deep breath, steeled himself, and slowly stepped out of the door and onto the side of the train. He inched along the walls of *The Astrolabe,* digging his fingers into the sheets of white metal. His arms strained to keep himself upright.

"Be careful!" Cole yelled over the roar of the wind.

"OK, that's far enough! You made it!" Mrs. Cunningham said as Gabe paused to catch his breath in the middle of the third train compartment from the front. "Now, slide under the train, find the green lever, and pull it towards you!"

Gabe looked down at the swirling abyss beneath him and his legs started shaking – if he fell, it would be very uncomfortable getting pulled back into *The Astrolabe*. He grimaced, his heart pounding in his chest, and then he lowered his foot and began to carefully climb underneath *The Astrolabe*. It wasn't easy, and his hands slipped on the metal walls several times, but the nylon rope kept him steady.

When Gabe had managed to pull the lower half of his body underneath the train, a dazzling bolt of lightning suddenly rained down and struck the air close to the train. Like a yawning mouth, another separate wormhole opened, and yet another chaotic scene was unfolding: everyone could see a beach with blood-soaked sand, and the sky above it was a somber grey color. Hundreds of uniformed soldiers that were holding heavy guns jumped out of boats and ran up the sand. They dodged Czech hedgehogs and barbed wire as the sound of rapid gunfire echoed out of the wormhole.

"Watch out!" Cole screamed. His eyes bulged in terror as a blast of gunfire suddenly exited the separate wormhole and struck the exterior of *The Astrolabe.* Deep puncture wounds riddled the metal walls.

"Where is Gabe?!" Brody cried.

Silence fell as the wormhole closed and disappeared. The only sound that Cole could hear was the wind rushing past the train.

"I…I don't see him!" he groaned.

A moment later, a hand appeared from underneath the train and waved.

"I'M OK!" Gabe's voice shouted. Everyone on the train breathed a sigh of relief.

Gabe continued moving underneath the train, hanging from a row of metal bars above him as if he was crossing a set of monkey bars on a playground, until he approached the green lever. He held his arm out, reaching for the lever, but his fingers missed it. Once. Twice. Three times.

"Dammit!" he yelled, sweat pouring down his face.

Gabe readjusted his position, and, with one final reach, he stretched out his hand and it finally folded over the lever. He yanked it towards himself and *The Astrolabe* groaned and shuddered.

"HE DID IT!" Mrs. Cunningham cheered. She rushed to the main control panel, flipped a switch, and, at long last, *The Astrolabe* finally began to slow down.

As Gabe was making his way back, random items from the 1770's began to float through the air: copies of the Declaration of Independence swam by like a school of fish; a painting of a young Marie Antoinette lightly bounced off his back; off in the distance, James Cook's wooden ship, the HMS Endeavor, sailed by. Samuel Adams was so shocked by the floating items that his eyes rolled back and he fainted.

By the time that Gabe jumped back into the front train compartment, the lightning storm finally stopped. Cole ran up to him and gave him a long hug. Moments later, *The Astrolabe* pulled to a stop in front of the 1770's Decade Station.

CHAPTER SEVENTEEN

Cole, Gabe, Brody, and an unconscious Samuel sank through the 1770's wormhole before finally landing in an empty graveyard. The churning sky above them was pearl white and so low that it felt like a ceiling. A thick elm tree towered over them, its long, bare branches creating a spindly, wooden awning over their heads. Next to the cemetery was a large grain storage building. Its roof was covered in thick, white snow.

"Come on, Samuel, wake up!" Brody said. He leaned down and slapped Samuel across the face.

"Wh-What?" Samuel cried. He sat up and looked around in confusion. "Where are we?"

"You fainted, but don't worry. We're back in Boston."

"What happened? I remember strange objects floating in the air...and then everything faded to black..."

"Floating objects? Oh, you were probably just dreaming! Can you walk?" Brody grabbed Samuel's hands and slowly helped him to his feet.

"Come on, let's get you to the Old South Meeting House," Cole said.

"The sun is setting. We must hurry," Samuel said. "Everyone will be looking for me. If we don't do something to show Parliament that they don't own us anymore, I fear that things will only get worse for the colonies."

They wound their way through the large graveyard, walking past stubby gray tombstones that dotted the snowy area, before exiting through a rusty gate and hurrying down the frigid streets of colonial Boston. They followed Samuel down Bromfield Street, passing through the young and emerging city.

A wall of red brick Georgian-style houses and wooden pubs ran along both sides of the street. Samuel led them past cobblestone alleyways and snow-covered wagons, dodging groups of women wearing white caps and blue cotton dresses who were making their way through the cold city. Cole shivered and pulled his tricorn hat down over his eyes to block the freezing wind.

"How much further?" Brody asked, his teeth chattering.

"Nearly there!" Samuel answered.

After taking a left onto a wide street, they spotted a red brick church off in the distance, the largest building in all of colonial Boston. The Old South Meeting House had a triangular roof that was blanketed with snow, as well as a one hundred- and eighty-three-foot-tall steeple that reached for the sky; the top of it was a forest green color. A massive crowd of thousands of men, women, and children were standing in front of the entrance to the church.

The now familiar flash of white light suddenly filled the air, knocking people to their knees, and then abruptly disappeared. A fiery rush of excitement rolled through Cole's body, and tears filled his eyes – they had finally done it! All they had to do was close the tear in time and they would be free!

"Well, Samuel, I think it's time that we took our leave," he said. "We have to get back to our work –"

"No, you mustn't leave!" Samuel cried. "As members of the Sons of Liberty, you have to attend this meeting. You saved my life, so it would mean quite a lot to me if you stayed." And, without waiting for an answer, he grabbed Cole's arm and dragged him over to the church, Gabe and Brody following close behind.

The three boys could feel rage radiating off the crowd like waves of heat. Shouts of anger filled the air as a dramatic confrontation unfolded in front of them. A dozen brutish guards, all of them wearing white wigs and blood red livery coats, were roughly lining up members of the crowd and slapping chains on their wrists.

"What are those guards doing?!" Cole cried.

"The red coats are trying to put a stop to this meeting!" Samuel answered.

The agitated crowd continued to shout, swaying from side to side as they pushed and shoved against the guards. Unfortunately, muskets with bayonets were being pointed directly at their faces, so they couldn't take any further action.

"Unhand them!" Samuel yelled, and he ran towards the guards in red coats and started swinging his fists. Gabe, Brody, and Cole ran after him. They punched and shoved the guards in red coats, and, once the colonists in the crowd noticed the brawl taking place, they stopped what they were doing and joined in the fight.

Samuel Adams was fearless – with no thought for his own safety, he slammed his body into the closest guard and wrestled him to the ground. The guard's musket fired, ringing sharply in the winter air. Samuel emerged unscathed, however, and, with a quick punch to the guard's face, he knocked him unconscious.

As soon as all of the guards had been dispatched, a cheer rang out from the crowd. Cole smiled, and, despite the bloody cut that now rested above his eyebrow, he remained in good spirits --

the electrifying energy from the surrounding colonists was infectious.

"Listen to me, fellow countrymen and citizens of Boston!" Samuel cried out. He raced to the top of the stairs in front of the Old South Meeting House. A hush fell over the crowd.

"I want to sincerely thank you, all of you, for assembling here this evening. You are a strong and proud people, and I am humbled to be in your presence.

Now, I must reiterate what is at stake tonight. I am sure that you are all aware of the Tea Act. The East India Company, that ruthless arm of the British Empire, wants to create a monopoly on the sale of tea – our merchants will suffer from this! They will not be able to provide for their families. We *cannot* allow Parliament to conspire to impose yet another tax on us when we have no voice in government. The Townsend Acts were a treacherous beginning, but these new taxes are a step too far. No taxation without representation!"

"Hear hear!" a man at the front of the crowd yelled.

"And you mustn't forget what happened in the year of our Lord seventeen hundred and seventy! That senseless and horrific murder of our citizens, in cold blood, by British soldiers! Your liberty and freedom were at stake then, and they are still at stake now! But, when we come together, we can accomplish anything. We demanded the complete withdrawal of troops, and it came to fruition! We opposed the Stamp Act, and we will also oppose the Tea Act. Like a once proud parent that has become consumed with hatred and avarice, the Crown is trying to punish us. We cannot allow this to stand. So, I must urge you now to continue to defy it. Where the law ends, tyranny begins!"

As he stood in front of the crowd with a determined expression on his face, something inside of him seemed to expand and a transformation took place. What once seemed to be just a small and unassuming man, in his place stood the fierce leader that the three boys had read about in history books; he seemed to have grown several inches in height. It was clear that he had a strong influence over the crowd.

"We have received word that Governor Hutchinson is refusing to send those infernal ships away, so we must take matters into our own hands! This meeting can do nothing further to save this country. Who will follow me to the harbor?"

The colonists roared their approval, screaming and clapping loudly. The same look of steely determination was reflected on everyone's faces.

Suddenly, the crowd swelled around Cole, pushing him forward as Gabe and Brody were swept away in a different direction.

"Wait, come back!" he yelled, but he had no choice but to let the current take him.

For the next ten minutes, the massive crowd rushed toward Boston Harbor. Cole's ears were filled with the sounds of laughter and bawdy songs being sung by a group of young men walking next to him. Off in the distance, above a line of wooden buildings, he could just make out white sails.

Like a tidal wave crashing onto a beach, the massive crowd finally poured onto the long harbor and made their way to the tip of the wooden dock. Many of the colonists were now holding lit torches or cloth signs that had the words, "No Taxation Without Representation!" painted on them. Cole's eyes widened in surprise when he saw an effigy of a British soldier that had been lit on fire – these people were not messing around.

The dark and icy waters of the Massachusetts Bay extended around the harbor for miles, splashing against the hulls of several large, wooden ships that dotted the bay, their white sails flapping in the strong breeze. The darkening sky stretched out above them.

"Dump the bloody tea!" someone in the crowd yelled.

With a loud roar, hundreds of men wearing disguises suddenly clambered onto three nearby ships. They were all dressed like Mohawk warriors, large headdresses on their heads and colorful paint on their faces.

These men pulled themselves up the tall bulkheads until they finally reached the ship decks. Hundreds of wooden crates that contained tea had been placed in large stacks throughout the ships. The disguised protestors rushed up to the crates, picked them up, and triumphantly tossed them into the dark water. The crowd of colonists along the harbor cheered as the crates hit the bay with a loud splash and broke open, scattering tea leaves across the dark surface of the water. One by one, each of the three hundred and forty-two tea crates was tossed into Massachusetts Bay.

"Cole! Hey, Cole!"

Gabe, with Brody following behind, pushed his way through the crowd and came up to Cole. "There you are! We've been looking everywhere for you. How crazy is this?"

More shouts of excitement rippled through the crowd. Cole, Brody, and Gabe hugged each other and cheered with everyone. Getting to experience this major moment in American history was heady and surreal.

Samuel suddenly appeared in the crowd, waving at them.

"My dear friends! Have you ever seen anything as exciting as this?!"

"We can't say that we have!" Cole replied, smiling widely.

"I wanted to thank you for bringing me back to Boston," Samuel said. "We would not have been able to accomplish this victory without you. How can I ever repay you?"

"There's no need to repay us! We're just happy that we could help. Just continue doing what you're doing and that will be enough for us," Gabe answered warmly.

"Oh, I can assure you that I will never give up! Now, if you ever find yourself in need of any assistance with the Sons of Liberty demonstrations, you know where to find me."

The boys waved, turned around, and made their way back to the Granary Burying Ground. Cole walked with a cheerful bounce in his step, ready to finally end this mission once and for all.

CHAPTER EIGHTEEN

Ruby moved to the window and stared through the large pane of glass, looking down at the silent streets far below. The sun was just beginning to rise in the distance; the sky looked like a black cloth that was slowly being dyed light blue.

Any minute now, she thought, looking down at her watch. This had to be done properly.

Ruby moved away from the window and began to pace back and forth, her thoughts spinning wildly. She was moving through an empty office, one of many that were inside an office building that had been abandoned. A jagged hole had been blown through a wall in the office, and a strong breeze blew inside and tousled her blonde hair. This location had been chosen because of the wide avenue that ran in front of it; it was essential to her plan.

After Karma left her at the Cheswick Hotel, Ruby sat down on Gustav's bed and cried harder than she had cried in years. Waves of rejection and disappointment vibrated through her body like soundwaves in a cave, making her want to curl up and hide away from the world. *How could Karma abandon me? Why would she give up?* She thought that Karma understood that this wasn't over until Project Hominum was punished and, ultimately, destroyed.

After an hour of crying herself hoarse, she removed her hands from her face and, with a shuddering breath, stared at the floor in a daze. Alone and miserable, she had no other choice but to retreat to Arthur's house and wait until everyone returned. So, she picked herself up, wiped her face, and walked dejectedly out of the hotel.

For the next two hours, Ruby walked slowly down the broken streets of Mechanica City, her scattered thoughts pinging around inside her mind. Her back and chest burned uncomfortably, both riddled with tension and exhaustion. She looked around at her dismal surroundings and a flower of despair bloomed larger and larger in her heart.

I've accomplished nothing. Nothing has changed. I'm a failure.

She walked past a large silver library and came upon a street that was bordered on both sides by a collection of run-of-the-mill shops.

Ruby abruptly stopped in her tracks. Something wasn't right. Several feet away, a pile of *something,* possibly clothes, was laying in the middle of the street, but she was too far away to determine what it was. The pile of what looked like clothes shuddered and twitched strangely.

As she slowly approached the mysterious clothing pile, the fabric fluttering in a strong breeze, her vision became clearer and she realized that it wasn't clothes that she was looking at, but, rather, two mechanicals, a man and a woman, who were dressed in traveling attire. Suitcases were strewn on the ground next to them. The woman's leg was twitching.

"Excuse me. Are you alright?" Ruby asked.

The mechanicals didn't respond.

"Hello? Do you need help?"

Only silence answered her. Confused and full of dread, Ruby walked up to the man and woman and stood over them. With a gasp, she clapped her hands to her mouth and reeled back in horror -- the mechanicals were both dead! Their heads had been torn off and placed next to their metal corpses. Someone had spray painted the letters PH across their backs – this was Project Hominum's doing.

Spots started popping in front of Ruby's eyes as a wave of fiery rage rolled through her. She collapsed to the ground and gaped at the bodies.

This can't be allowed to happen! No, this can't go unpunished, she thought, and tears started pouring down her face. These mechanicals, who did nothing to cause this, were just trying to escape the city and someone had brutally murdered them. They were the unlucky ones who had ended up on this particular street, on this particular day, at the absolute worst time. The metal carnage lying at her feet tore at her insides and she released a roar of frustration that echoed down the street. How much more senseless violence would she have to bear witness to because of Project Hominum? She felt lost and helpless.

She reached into her pocket for a tissue to wipe her eyes and her hand grazed the USB drive. She froze in shock as she was struck by a sudden realization.

You idiot! she chastised herself. She had been so distracted ever since Karma had left her that she had completely forgotten about the Project Hominum index. She wasn't helpless after all! She had everything that she needed.

With a new sense of purpose pulsing through her, Ruby wiped her eyes, got to her feet, and turned in a slow circle, analyzing her surroundings. Standing next to a line of silver high rises off in the distance, she found what she was looking for -- an MCPD station; there were dozens scattered throughout the city. She could still bring down Project Hominum, she would just need some different help. Thinking outside of the box was what was required now.

Ten minutes later, with determination burning in her chest, Ruby rushed into Mechanica

City Police Station #3927. The main lobby was quiet and still, and her boots squeaked against the glossy marble floor. A pair of gruff police officers, one with freckles and the other with bright pink lipstick, eyed her carefully as she approached their cluttered desk.

"I-I, um, need to speak to the police chief. It's an emergency."

"What do you want?" the guard with the freckles asked.

Ruby took a deep, steadying breath before saying, "You have to listen to me. I really need to speak to the police chief."

"And why is that, ma'am? He's a very busy man and can't be bothered with silly requests," the guard with the bright pink lipstick barked.

"Do you want to take down Project Hominum once and for all? Because I can tell you the identity of every single member, living or dead. I have an up to date index."

The guard with the freckles scoffed. "Don't be ridiculous. That's impossible."

"Why do you say that?"

"Well, because if a resource like that actually existed, the MCPD would already have it. Now, please leave."

"No offense, but the MCPD isn't always the most, you know, *informed.*"

The guards glared at her.

Ruby decided to change tactics. "Fine! Don't believe me? Look at this."

She made to move around the desk, but the guards jumped out of their chairs in surprise and pointed their guns at her.

"Get back!"

"Don't shoot! I'm not crazy and I'm not making this up!" Ruby cried, putting her hands in the air. "Just let me show you my USB drive."

"Why should we trust you?" the guard with the lipstick asked.

An uncomfortable shard of anxiety grew in Ruby's stomach. *Have I made the wrong decision?* she wondered. But competing emotions, anger and determination, began to bounce around in her mind, and she realized that she had to be strong, stronger than she'd ever been in her life. She couldn't allow herself to give up on this.

"I'm going to reach into my –" she started to say.

"Hey! What are you doing?" the guard with pink lipstick yelled.

"Can I grab my phone? I just want to show you a picture." Ruby slowly reached into her pants pocket and pulled out her phone. She wasn't exactly keen on using this "card," but desperate times call for desperate measures.

"You see this? This is a picture of me and my dad. This is Arthur Bennett. You know, the famous inventor? Yeah, I'm his daughter."

The guard with the freckles lowered his gun and then peered at Ruby's phone. "Hmm…you're the daughter of that guy who saved everyone during The Malick Scandal?"

"Exactly, so, how do you think it will look if you were to injure his daughter? You would get in serious trouble. So, can you just chill out? I'm not going to do anything suspicious. Just look at the information that I have and then you can make your decision."

The two guards looked at each other, shrugged, and then put their guns back in their holsters. Ruby moved quickly to the desk and started typing feverishly on a keyboard. They stared at her skeptically, but, after she inserted the USB drive into the port and pulled up an organized database of names with corresponding photos, including snippets from wiretapped phone calls, they quickly let go of their trepidation and warmed up to her. Video evidence of maskless Project Hominum members committing various crimes moved across the computer screen.

"My boss is definitely going to want to see this," the guard with the pink lipstick said, an awestruck expression on her face.

Fifteen minutes later, a man with sandy blonde hair and a face that was angular and attractive strode through the front doors of the police station. Ruby felt mildly shocked to see that he was young, probably around her age. His facial expression was serious, but his eyes were warm.

"Sorry to bother you, Commissioner Carpenter," the guard with the lipstick said, "but this is the lady that I told you about."

"You must be Ruby," Commissioner Carpenter said, extending his hand. "Call me Orlando."

When Ruby's hand touched his, a warm tingle radiated through her hand and she blushed. "N-Nice to meet you, sir."

"What can I do for you? I hear that you've got something important to show me."

"Yes. I've come into possession of some incredibly damning evidence concerning Project Hominum, and I want every member arrested and sent away. You can make that happen for me."

Orlando's eyes widened in surprise -- he clearly wasn't expecting this answer.

"Really? How did you get something like that?"

"It's a long story."

"Well...we've been hoping for something like this for weeks. Why don't I take you to my office and you can start from the beginning?"

For the next several hours, Ruby and Orlando sat behind his computer and poured over the Project Hominum database. Row after row of names and faces, a few of which were well known to Orlando, flashed by them. Every time he recognized someone, he groaned and shook his head in disgust.

Ruby was shocked at how easily she found herself warming up to this man, a complete stranger to her. Working with him and opening up about everything that she had been through somehow felt both natural and easy. Although Orlando was reserved and focused on the task at hand, Ruby could sense that there was a fierce intellect and a warmth there. Together, they ended up piecing together a trap for Project Hominum. Their plan was simple, but, if done right, it would be extremely effective.

"OK. So, at sunrise, my team and I will wait for you at the designated spot," Orlando said.

"Excellent," Ruby answered. "And you have my number in case there are any issues."

"Thank you again for bringing this to the attention of the MCPD. Mechanica City owes you a debt of gratitude. Thanks to you, there's a good chance that we'll finally be able to take down Project Hominum."

Ruby smiled, waved, and then left the police station.

Back at the office building, she continued pacing up and down the dark office, periodically checking her watch. *Not too much longer now,* she thought. Her heart started pounding in her chest.

She sat down in a chair behind a mahogany desk, and, for a brief moment, allowed her thoughts to wander. She wondered what she would do when all of this was over. Going back to being a dancer seemed impossible after everything that had happened. What did she want to do with her life? What was next? If this plan went off without a hitch, the possibilities would be endless.

Her pants pocket vibrated. Ruby pulled out her phone and answered the call.

"Hey. Is everyone in position?"

"Yes ma'am. Armed and ready," Orlando's voice answered.

Ruby moved to the window again and looked out. If she squinted hard enough, she could now just barely make out armed police officers kneeling on the roofs of the surrounding buildings. Heavy rifles rested on their shoulders, and the barrels were pointed at the avenue below.

"You're sure that they're going to show up?" Orlando asked.

"Oh, they definitely will. I'll make sure of it."

"Good. Now, I also wanted to ask...are you ready for this?"

"You have no idea. More than I can say."

He cleared his throat uncomfortably. "Well...you know...just be careful, OK?"

A small smile crawled up her face and she blushed deeply.

"I will." She hung up.

An alarm buzzed on her watch – it was time. Ruby picked up Gustav's Project Hominum mask and pressed the mouthpiece for five seconds. It glowed and she felt a vibration go through her hand.

"Attention: this is Gustav Fallowback speaking," she said, using a voice changing app on her phone to deepen her voice. "I have returned. All members of Project Hominum must report to 157 East Parsons Avenue at once, or you will be punished. A new opportunity has emerged."

When the mask finally stopped glowing, she slipped into a bulky jacket and pulled her hair into a ponytail. With a deep, steadying breath, she moved to the window to watch everything unfold.

Like water dripping slowly out of a sink, the minutes crawled by. Ruby stood rooted to the floor, watching for any sign of Project Hominum. Nothing was happening.

Come on... she thought. Her heart was pounding in her chest. *Where are these bastards?*

Down below, there was a flicker of movement. Holding up a pair of binoculars, she peered through the lenses and watched as a masked Project Hominum member came into view and slowly moved across the wide avenue. They paused, looked around to see if anyone was watching, and then, when the coast was clear, they continued to cautiously approach the office building.

Soon, a few more people showed up, all of them wearing masks. They came out of doorways and from behind shadowy street corners. A crowd started to form, and it grew and expanded until more than seventy people were standing in front of the nondescript office building. A sea of expressionless Project Hominum masks greeted Ruby; it was an unnerving sight. Most of the crowd was either streaked with dirt, bloody from injuries, or a combination of both.

"Gustav, we're here!" yelled a Project Hominum member.

Here we go, Ruby thought. She slipped the Project Hominum mask over her face and shivered with disgust. Then, she opened the window, and, using the voice changing app, she spoke into a microphone and addressed the crowd below.

"My family! Thank you for meeting me here. You should feel very proud, for you are true believers!"

"Where is Jaxon? We have witnesses who saw him disappear!" another member cried.

"Allow me to explain," Ruby answered. "I'm sorry to say that he has been killed."

"No!" someone in the crowd shouted.

"Arthur Bennett's disgusting family murdered him in cold blood!"

"Is that really you, Gustav? How can this be?" a Project Hominum member shouted.

"I thought it best if I disappeared for some time. My enemies were after me and I didn't want to take any chances. I've been traveling the country, regrouping and building up our support. I have something new in store!

Mechanica City has been conquered. Despite our failure to prevent mechanicals from being created, our noble actions have still managed to destroy much of the city. It's broken and defenseless. We will take it over by force and create our very own utopia, a brand-new city where humans can thrive and be free from machines! No more hiding and no more deception. Now is the time to take bold action. Here is what I need you to do – give into your hatred. Let it overwhelm you. Roam the streets and kill every mechanical that you see. One way or another, we will finally destroy them once and for all!"

The Project Hominum members cheered, pumping their fists in the air.

"On the count of three! One...two...three!"

Ruby shielded her eyes as bright spotlights abruptly came to life. With an exploding sound, thick nylon nets blasted out of large gun barrels and rained down onto the crowd, knocking people to the ground and holding them fast. Hundreds of police officers in bulky black riot gear poured onto the wide avenue, handguns drawn and ready. Some of the Project Hominum members tried to run, or shoot at the police, but, like a tidal wave, the officers crashed into them and quickly overtook them. Bronze jail dirigibles descended from the sky and landed in the street.

Loud noises popped around Ruby. As if she was listening to a vibrant symphony, she closed her eyes and let the panicked cries of the Project Hominum members surround her -- it was the sound of justice being served. Euphoria rushed through her body, lighting her up like fireworks. Her plan had worked!

Tears suddenly flooded her eyes, and Ruby leaned against a wall and sobbed loudly into her hands. It felt like a dam had broken and burst open within her, and all her stress poured out of her. It was finally over – Project Hominum couldn't hurt her or anyone else anymore. She was safe. She was free.

She walked slowly down a cement stairwell, blood pounding in her ears, and then opened a door that led out of the office building. The sun was just beginning to rise in the sky, and Ruby felt its warm beams pass over her. Despite the exhaustion that clung to her, she felt happy.

"Miss Bennett!"

Ruby turned her head and saw Orlando pushing his way across the chaotic avenue. He jumped out of the way as a guard slammed a masked man against a jail dirigible and then he ran up to her.

"Are you OK, ma'am?"

She wiped her eyes and smiled. "I-I'm wonderful, Orlando. Just, you know, feeling a little overwhelmed."

Orlando smiled widely and shook her hand. "You should be very proud of yourself! Look at what you've accomplished! Project Hominum has been defeated. Mechanica City owes you a debt of gratitude! Please, let me do something for you. Can you let me and my team members get you breakfast? I'm sure you could use a pick-me-up."

Ruby's face slowly lit up with a large smile. "A group of handsome men want to buy me breakfast? Don't mind if I do!"

CHAPTER NINETEEN

"Alright, guys, we're here. The last task," Gabe said. The three boys were standing in front of a glowing Time Screen.

"It feels great to hear that said out loud," Brody replied with a wide smile. "Now, do we have all of the equipment that we need?"

"Hmm...we've got our blasters, radios, and the pocket watch. Am I forgetting anything?" Gabe asked.

"Oh, and I've got the Gödel Brush," Cole said.

"That should be everything!" Gabe said. He turned to the Time Screen, typed a date onto the glass surface, and took a step back. In the air directly in front of them, a wormhole unzipped itself and fell open. The boys ran and jumped into it.

After slowly sinking through the folds of time, Cole, Gabe, and Brody were spit out of a portal and they landed on the cold, hard floor of a dark cave. Soft light poured in from the mouth of the cave, and Cole could just make out green grass blowing in the wind.

As they got to their feet, a chirping sound came from the shadowy back corner of the cave.

Three small creatures, a trio of *Oryctodromeus* dinosaurs, suddenly emerged from the shadows and approached the three boys. They walked on two hind legs, and their green, leathery bodies were covered in rippling patterns. Like a group of dogs, they chirped and sniffed at the boy's ankles.

"Aww. So cute! Come here, little babies," Brody gushed. He smiled and held out his hand.

"Umm. I don't know if you should do that..." Gabe warned.

A thunderous roar ripped through the silence, raising the hair on the back of everyone's necks. Out of the murky darkness stepped a much larger *Oryctodromeus;* its pointed head nearly came up to Cole's chest. The creature stood for a moment, teeth bared, its shrewd, golden eyes taking them all in, before it opened its wide mouth, lined with rows of jagged fangs, and released another bone-chilling roar.

"Th-That must be the mother! RUNNN!" Cole screamed.

The boys turned and raced towards the cave entrance, their shoes pounding against the stone floor, as the large *Oryctodromeus* bounded after them, its massive jaws snapping at their heels.

"Is *The Astrolabe* trying to get us killed?!" Brody cried.

At the last second, right before sharp teeth sank into their flesh, they threw themselves out of the mouth of the cave and landed roughly in the dirt. The angry dinosaur skidded to a halt at the entrance and bared her teeth. Then, after one final roar, she turned and nudged her children back inside the cave.

"Wh...What the hell was that all about?" Gabe cried.

"We better start being extra cautious while we're here," Cole answered.

The boys got to their feet and took a moment to take in their lush and verdant surroundings. They were standing on an outcropping that jutted out from the side of a jagged mountain face. Far below, a sloshing river wound its way towards a thick forest of ginkgo trees that stood off in the distance. Thick green grass covered the ground for miles in every direction. The air was thick with humidity, making everyone feel like they had just stepped into a sauna. A pale blue sky wobbled and churned above their heads.

Above the dark green treetops of the gingko forest, the boys could just make out flashes of lightning.

"Look, there's the Time Tear!" Cole said, pointing down at the forest. "It's only a couple of miles away, but stay alert and focused. We'll almost certainly see more dinosaurs on the way."

For the next hour, Cole, Brody, and Gabe slowly made their way down the side of the mountain. They walked by swaths of overgrown plants with uniquely-shaped leaves: massive ferns, patches of branched horsetails with dense cones that were almost like crowns, and stubby *Williamsonia*. Neon pink flowers grew alongside pungent trees with thick trunks. Cycads with wide palms were bountiful, along with bright green conifer trees. Brody took a deep breath of the floral, pungent air.

Despite the lush and beautiful nature that surrounded him, a cloying sense of unease began to creep into Cole's mind. This place held many conflicting memories for him, and he never imagined that he would ever set foot here again. Yet here he was.

Let's get this over with, he thought.

"Man...when this is all over, I really hope that Nautique is still standing. I can't wait to get back. It's going to take so much work to get us back to where we used to be," Gabe said. "What about you guys? Do you have any plans after we return to Mechanica City?"

Cole and Brody were silent while they considered his question. The past few weeks had been full of struggle, and their thoughts had been so jumbled and confusing, that neither of them had spent much time thinking about what would happen in the upcoming months.

"Well...to start with, there's graduation," Cole finally answered. "Assuming Brume University is even standing anymore. Finishing up classes and final exams."

"Moving in with me," Gabe said, smiling.

Cole blushed. "Yes, moving in with you. And then I have to figure out a way to get a job, since Technicus Incorporated didn't work out. I've been hesitant to really think about this. I'll be honest -- even before that whole Oscar Wilde situation, I just wanted everything to stay the way it was. The past two years have been so amazing...my father returning, being with you...it makes me sad to think that everything will change again."

"Don't worry, you'll find a job, Cole," Gabe said. "You're smart and skilled at what you do, so something will turn up. But as for the other stuff...well... you're right. Things will be changing soon. But not everything. Not the important things. And besides, being out of school isn't bad! I've had a pretty great time so far."

"It's like Josephine Baker said. Life only moves in one direction, and that's forward. The past is the past, and, as we've seen, there's nothing we can do to change it or relive it. College is almost over," Brody said. "We'll just have to make the most of it while it lasts. And at least we're going through it together."

Cole was silent for several minutes, absorbing what they had said. They were absolutely right -- trying to fight change would only hurt him in the long run. Successfully moving through life involved adapting and always looking forward.

"Brody, you seem clear on what you're doing. New York City will be lucky to have you," Gabe said.

Brody sighed and looked down at the ground. A bright red blush burned on his pale cheeks.

"Listen...I owe you both an apology. When I said that I couldn't wait to move to New York City and get away from you? I didn't mean that. You're my closest friends, and I...I'm sorry that I said that." His chin wobbled and he wiped away tears that had pooled in his eyes.

"It's OK, Brody," Cole said. "You were just upset. And I'm sorry that you were forced to go on this mission. I shouldn't have ignored your feelings."

"Well...none of that petty drama matters now. We're about to finish this mission and go back home. And besides, this has actually been an amazing adventure! I'll probably never get to experience time travel again after this, so I should try to embrace it."

When the boys finally reached the bottom of the mountain, they headed north and walked across a wide and rolling valley that led towards the forest.

Tall, thin trees with large, glossy leaves dotted the grassy landscape.

Before they had made it halfway across the sloping valley, the ground beneath their feet began to shake.

"What's happening?!" Brody yelled.

Off in the distance, a small herd of long-necked dinosaurs suddenly broke through the gingko forest and started moving across the valley. Cole, Gabe, and Brody gasped and stared in wonder; the size of the creatures took their breath away. It was a family of four brontosauruses, each one the size of a small apartment building, and they moved slowly on four massive feet. Their textured skin was a mottled grey color.

"Am I really seeing this?" Brody asked in disbelief.

Goosebumps ran up and down Cole's arms as he gawked at the slow-moving dinosaur herd. The towering creatures were gentle and relaxed, barely noticing the boys as they paused to munch on leaves that rested at the top of the thin trees.

When the three boys finally approached the edge of the gingko forest, Cole's pants pocket started talking.

"Hello? Cole? Can you hear me? Testing. 1, 2, 3."

"Is that Karma's voice?" Brody asked in shock.

Cole yanked the radio out of his pocket. "Karma? Is that you?!"

"Yes, it's me! I'm so happy to hear from you!" her voice cried. "I've reached out so many times, but I never got an answer!"

"Something must be wrong with our radios. I've been so worried about you! How are you and Ruby? Oh, and how is Mechanica City?"

"The city is still in rough shape, but I'm doing fine. Your sister should be fine, too!"

"Should be? You don't know?"

"Well, um, she's still in Mechanica City. We actually discovered a database that has information about every member of Project Hominum. I know that she has everything under control. She'll be fine!"

"Wait...you left her?"

"It's a really long story. I'll explain everything later."

Cole frowned. Why did she abandon Ruby? Did something happen in Mechanica City? However, in order to stay focused on the task at hand, he stayed silent.

"Anyway...I'm almost to the Mesozoic Era. I figured that you guys would probably be there at this point," Karma said.

"We are. You might miss us sealing the Time Tear, but we'll take *The Astrolabe* back together if that happens."

"OK, I'll see you soon!"

Cole sighed heavily and put the radio back in his pants pocket. "That conversation was weird, right?"

"Hmm..." Brody mumbled. "It *is* a little weird that she seemingly abandoned Ruby. But...maybe she has a reasonable explanation."

The boys entered the ginkgo forest. Their boots crunched against tree berries as they passed by large, fan-shaped leaves, pushing them aside so that they could see better. Sturdy tree trunks, covered in thick vines, dotted the path forward, and a sharp and acidic smell filled their nostrils. Cole wiped the sweat off his forehead; the air in the forest was stifling.

"Do you hear that?" Gabe asked, stopping in his tracks.

The boys paused to listen. They could hear a faint howling noise, like the groaning winds of a hurricane, coming from somewhere deep in the forest.

"We're nearly there. Let's keep moving," Cole said.

Fifteen minutes later, Brody, Gabe, and Cole pushed past a cluster of tree branches and finally came upon the other side of the forest. They gasped and reeled back in shock – the Time Tear was enormous, and it looked like it had gotten much larger since they had last seen it. Gale-force winds were being sucked into the massive tear, creating a loud *whoosh* noise that made the air vibrate. At the center of the tear churned a violent orange light that swirled and thrummed, bright as the Sun.

The boys approached the tear, making sure that they didn't get too close. Cole took a deep, steadying breath and pulled out the Gödel Brush.

"Here we go!" he yelled over the wind. Holding the brush in his hands, pulse quickening, he turned and aimed it at the edge of the Time Tear.

"Now what?" Brody asked.

"There's a button on the bottom," Cole explained. "Let me just push it, and --"

He was roughly thrown off his feet as a ropy energy blast shot straight out of the glittery bristles of the paintbrush and attached to the tear. It vibrated heavily in his hands, but he managed to hold it steady.

However, after a few seconds, the energy blast sputtered, made a sad whining sound, and then fizzled out completely.

"What happened?" Gabe asked.

"I...I don't know! It's not working," Cole said.

Suddenly, a sound like fluttering feathers filled the boy's ears and Thelonia appeared in the air in front of them. She glowed brightly. Through squinted eyes, the boys could see that she had a smirk on her face.

"Thelonia, what are you doing here?" Brody asked.

"Can you help us? The Gödel Brush isn't working!" Cole cried.

Thelonia laughed. "Of course it isn't!"

CHAPTER TWENTY

"What are you talking about?" Cole asked.

"The paintbrush doesn't work like that," Thelonia said.

"But…that's what Aloicius told us."

"He did? Oh, right. I guess he made a mistake, didn't he?"

There was a strained silence. The three boys stared at her in confusion. What was she doing here? And why did she look so smug and defiant?

"Ok, well, how does it work then?" Cole asked. A sickly feeling of dread started to fill his stomach.

"The Time Tear can only be closed from the inside. That means that one of you will perish as you seal it," she answered bluntly.

"*WHAT?*" Gabe screamed.

"I know, it's very unfortunate. But it's for a noble cause! Now, you must hurry – if the tear reaches thirty feet across, it will break down and explode. All of reality will collapse."

From the depths of the Time Tear came a loud thunderclap. Jagged streaks of lightning exited the wormhole and flashed over their heads.

"Why didn't you tell us that before we started this mission?!" Cole yelled. He shook with rage as he struggled to comprehend everything that Thelonia was saying. *One of you will perish...*

Thelonia covered her mouth and giggled. It sounded strange and harsh, like dissonant piano keys. "You wouldn't have come if I had told you! And then my plan would've disintegrated."

"What plan? What are you talking about?" Brody asked.

Thelonia slowly floated down next to them. "Oh, just something that I've been working on for a long time. A *very* long time. And you're going to help me achieve it."

"We're not doing *anything* until you explain what the hell is going on!" Cole barked. "You're not making any sense!"

Thelonia's eyes flicked nervously to the Time Tear. "We don't have time for this!"

Cole crossed his arms and stared her down.

Thelonia's lip curled angrily and she sighed. "*Fine.* But I'll keep it brief -- I'm taking control of the Master Timeline, and you're going to help me do it. There. Can we stay focused now?"

"*What?!* Why would we agree to do that?" Gabe asked incredulously.

"You've been lying to us this whole time!" Brody snarled.

"Oh, don't be so naïve. You humans and your ridiculous morality. Yes, I lied. So what? You're still going to help me because you don't have a choice."

The three boys stared at her in horror, waiting for her to continue.

"Oh, don't look at me like that. Fine! I'll give you a little bit of context. I would be lying if I said that it doesn't feel good to talk about this. Hmm...where to start? During the first days of the Master Timeline, when the universe was amorphous and chaotic, I was brought into existence by Aloicius. Inside Atmos, he told me about my glorious purpose -- to observe the Timeline and ensure that its sacred flow was never disrupted. The centuries passed, and it was a peaceful and glorious time. I truly believed in what I was doing -- I was created for it, after all. I knew my purpose and I worked diligently."

"So...what changed?" Gabe asked softly.

"Well, I fell in love, that's what! And I got wrapped up in the insanity of the Time Conflict."

"The what?"

"Oh dear, I'm monologuing like a comic book villain, aren't I?" Thelonia muttered. She looked at the Time Tear nervously again before continuing her speech.

"I made the mistake of falling in love with a human woman. Her name was Petronilla and she was the most stunning creation that I've ever laid eyes on. Long, crimson hair…it took my breath away. Beautiful and smart. A *genius!* Unlike your father, she was *actually* the first person to create a time machine. Anyway, long story short, I broke the rules and got in trouble."

"What did you do?" Brody asked.

"IT DOESN'T MATTER!" she screamed, breathing hard. "It'll take too long to explain. Just know that the Master Timeline became untenable, so Aloicius reset it. Using a colossal amount of temporal energy, he ended all life and events in the Timeline and started everything over again."

"Everything just…disappeared?" Brody asked.

"Everything. Gone. No one to remember what happened. *No one to remember Petronilla!* This Master Timeline is the second one, not the first. I had spent centuries learning to love the humans that lived in that timeline, *so many years* following their lives, and all of it was ripped away from me!

When my fellow Uhrzeit discovered my 'treachery,' they had me captured and thrown into a prison cell. Bastards, all of them. But, I certainly got them back, didn't I? Anyway, I was forced to live in that cell for centuries, biding my time while I decided how I was going to respond to Aloicius. I was eventually released, but only because I successfully pretended to be rehabilitated." Thelonia chuckled darkly. "*Rehabiliated?* I don't think so. Not after what I had experienced. I will never be punished for refusing to be a passive observer again! There is no dignity in having no control over yourself or your surroundings!

After that business with Project Hominum and Oscar Wilde, Aloicius planned on resetting the Timeline once again. This time I was ready. I poisoned him, locked him away, and began the complicated process of absorbing his powers and knowledge. It's taken me a long time, for Aloicius is a very powerful being. But, once I take everything from him and we get the Time Tear sealed, I will control the Master Timeline. I will mold it to be the way that I want."

"But, your duty is to ensure that the Timeline unfolds without any distractions or roadblocks," Brody said. "You can't just do whatever you want. You'll destroy it!"

"See, that's where you're wrong," Thelonia said, smiling. "I can do whatever I want. I *will* take over. But, yes, if the Timeline collapses under my watch, then it collapses. At that point I won't care."

"You're insane!" Gabe cried.

"Don't call me that!" Thelonia screamed. A flickering streak of bright green energy exploded out of her hand and it went flying. The bolt of energy slashed Gabe across his left shoulder and arm, leaving a bloody gash. "I'm not insane! You have no right to judge me, you pathetic human!"

"GABE!" Cole screamed.

"The Elders will stop you!" Brody yelled.

"Oh, you stupid boy. There *are* no Elders. I've certainly never seen them. Only rumors."

The three boys stood in terrified silence. Their hearts were pounding in their chests, and they all felt nauseous. What were they going to do?

"You are a disgusting liar!" Brody screamed, turning to glare at Thelonia. "What the hell is wrong with you?!"

Thelonia chuckled. "I don't care that you hate me. You'll never understand my point of view because you are human beings and you have finite lives. I've existed for eternity. I've witnessed things that would drive you insane! But, enough of this! We're wasting time. One of you needs to close the Time Tear now!"

Hot tears poured down Cole's face, blurring his vision. His jagged thoughts spun wildly, and it felt like he was falling. There was no way out – they were trapped in a nightmare.

"Fine! I'll…I'll do it. Too many people are relying on us to get this done. Our families and friends. Everything that exists in the Master Timeline. If I do this, everyone will be safe."

"NO!" Gabe screamed. "None of us are doing that! We'll figure something out. Thelonia can go screw herself!"

Thelonia screamed in anger and rose into the air again. She lifted her hands and thick streams of fiery, crimson energy blasted out of her palms, tearing through the air like bolts of lightning, and struck the boys squarely in the chest. They were knocked off their feet and landed roughly on the ground; Cole felt the wind get knocked out of his lungs. The crimson energy blast molded itself around their bodies, encasing them like a shell, and they writhed in pain. Cole felt like flames were crawling all over his skin.

"ST-*STOPPPP!*" he screamed through gritted teeth. The force of the energy blast was keeping him pinned him to the ground, along with Brody and Gabe.

A freezing sensation started crawling up Cole's arm. When he looked down, his eyes bulged in horror as he realized that his arm was aging rapidly. Liver spots and wrinkles bloomed across the sagging skin.

Thelonia moved her right hand and Cole was yanked into the air. He floated in front of her, crying out in pain.

"You will seal the Time Tear *right now* or I will suck the life out of you!" Thelonia bellowed.

"*Put me down!*" Cole screamed. He looked down and saw that his other arm was starting to age rapidly now. What part of him would start aging next?

"LET THEM GO!"

Something moved at the corner of Cole's eye. A figure was running across the grass toward them.

"*I SAID LET THEM GO!*"

The figure pointed a blaster and fired off an energy bolt. It passed right through Thelonia's chest but made no damage. Cole's heart soared at the sound of the figure's voice – it was Karma!

CHAPTER TWENTY-ONE

As soon as Thelonia's eyes fell on Karma, the crimson energy bolts pouring out of her hands faded and Cole was released; he abruptly fell to the ground and landed with a *thud*.

"*What the hell are you doing?!*" Karma screamed. She clenched her fists and her brow furrowed in anger.

"It's…It's a trap!" Cole yelled. He slowly got to his feet. "The Time Tear will only close from the inside. Thelonia lied to us!"

"From the inside? What do you mea –"

"She wants to take over the Master Timeline!" Cole looked down and saw that his arms were slowly starting to de-age and return back to normal.

"BE QUIET!" Thelonia roared. She flicked her hand and sent a single crimson energy blast hurtling towards Cole. It struck him in the chest and sent him flying across the grass again. "But, yes, Cole is correct -- that's the gist of it."

"You're...You're INSANE!" Karma cried.

Thelonia laughed. "You may be right! However, that doesn't change the fact that you're powerless to stop me."

Suddenly, there was a great roaring sound as the Time Tear slowly began to expand. The jagged edges vibrated violently, reaching out horizontally and making the tear wider. The wind picked up and the orange crystals were yanked out of the ground and sucked into the tear. A deep crack formed on the ground.

"One of you better jump into the tear right now or I'll choose at random!" Thelonia screamed.

Karma turned her head and looked at the three boys with a solemn expression. Her chin wobbled and she used the back of her hand to wipe away tears.

"I'll do it," she said, her voice shaking.

"Karma, don't! You'll die!" Cole cried desperately.

"There's no other way," she said. Her face had crumpled and rivers of tears poured down her cheeks. "Just promise that you won't forget me."

"Do it now! Here is the Gödel Brush," Thelonia shrieked, and with a flick of her hand she sent the brush flying out of Cole's pocket and into

Karma's hand. With one last look at her friends, Karma sprinted towards the Time Tear.

"NOOOO!" Cole screamed.

When she was only a few feet from it, a strong gust of wind lifted her off the ground and pulled her into the Time Tear. Its interior churned with a throbbing orange light. She floated, hot wind blowing past her, and then she held out the paintbrush in front of her, pushed the button, and an energy blast shot out and struck the edges of the Time Tear. With a low groaning sound, the wormhole finally began to close.

"KARMA!" Brody yelled.

Karma watched the three boys from the other side of the wormhole, and the last thing they saw of her was her haunted expression as the Time Tear finally sealed shut.

Thelonia lowered her hands and Gabe and Brody were released from the crimson energy blasts. Cole fell to his knees and sobbed, devastated by the loss of his friend.

"You murdered our friend, you piece of trash!" Gabe screamed. He picked up a handful of rocks and started pelting them at her, but they went right through her.

Thelonia closed her eyes and let out a long sigh, a wicked smile on her face. "It is done. *At long last – I finally control all of reality!* Oh, it feels amazing to say that. Now, first things first: let's discuss your elimination."

"WHAT?!" Brody yelled.

"Yes, so sad. But I can't have you telling anyone what went into making my plan happen, can I? No, we can't have that. So, you will – hnkkk hnk! UGH!" Thelonia suddenly started clawing at her throat, eyes bulging in shock. Choking and sputtering, she sank to the ground.

A dense white fog started crawling across the grass. It filled the immediate area, swirling around everyone and clouding their vision.

"What's going on?" Cole asked.

Out of the fog stepped the strangest-looking group of people that the boys had ever seen, although it was debatable as to whether they could even be considered people. Twelve translucent spirits, clad in diaphanous robes that moved and fluttered around them, stepped forward, and resting above each of their shoulders, where a head and neck would normally be, were various items, ranging from animal faces to random objects: a noble lion with a golden mane, a fiery orange crab, a bug-eyed fish covered in scales, a pair of metal scales.

The three boys stared in shock at the bizarre humanoid beings as they silently walked toward Thelonia and formed a circle around her.

"Wh-Who are you? What do you want?" Thelonia asked. Her voice trembled with fear.

"We have been watching you, Thelonia. What we have seen has been very disappointing," one of the spirits said. It had the head of a scorpion.

Thelonia scowled, held up her hands, and released a torrent of black energy bolts. "Stay back! Don't come any closer!"

The bolts of energy passed through the transparent beings and struck a patch of grass behind them, causing them no bodily damage. Unfazed, they continued moving closer to her, closing in the circle, and then they held out their hands.

"NO! GET AWAY FROM ME!" Thelonia screamed, but there was nowhere for her to go. As soon as the mysterious spirits placed their hands on her, beams of bright, golden light erupted out of her chest and face. She threw her head back and screamed wildly, shaking and thrashing around, until the golden light beams enveloped her completely. By the time that the spirits lowered their hands, Thelonia had disappeared.

An ice-cold dagger of terror pierced Cole's insides as he stared at the circle of strange translucent spirits. What had they done to Thelonia? And were they going to do that to him?

One of the spirits, a humanoid being with the head of a shaggy ram with horns, started to approach him, but he scrambled backward in a panic.

"Are you boys alright?" the spirit asked. Their voice echoed softly, as if they were speaking from a great distance. "Don't worry, you're safe now. Thelonia is gone."

Gabe got off the ground and helped Brody and Cole to their feet.

"We...We're fine. I don't mean to be rude, but...what are you?" he asked nervously.

"Hmm...how shall I explain this? Our names are ancient; therefore, they simply cannot be understood by human minds or ears. But you may refer to us simply as The Elders. We have been watching you for many days, maintaining a discreet distance in order to observe your journey as it unfolded, as is our purview."

"Why are you here now?" Cole asked.

"We had no choice," the Elder with the lion head said. "Thelonia nearly succeeded in her nefarious scheme, and we couldn't allow that to happen. She nearly destroyed everything."

Cole's mind was jumbled, and blood pounded loudly in his ears. Nothing made sense. Karma was gone...Thelonia had been destroyed...The Master Timeline was safe. All of this in the span of a few minutes.

A rumbling noise suddenly filled the air. Everyone turned to look at a patch of air next to them that started wobbling and rippling. The twelve Elders stepped back in shock– something was coming.

Out of the wobbling air burst a pale white fist. It moved to the left and the right, opening a small hole. Then, another fist punched its way through. The two hands snatched at the rippling air, grabbed a fistful of it as if it was mere fabric, and pulled it apart, revealing a woman with white silicone skin and red hair…

"KARMA!" the three boys screamed.

Karma pushed her way through the ripples and tumbled through the air. However, instead of hitting the ground, she righted herself and started levitating; the tear that she had created closed behind her. Her hair gently floated around her as she slowly sank to the ground, and her eyes glowed with a soft, yellow light.

"Karma, we thought you were dead!" Cole cried. An explosion of relief flooded through his chest, and he felt dizzy and overwhelmed. "You saved the Master Timeline!"

The three boys ran to her and wrapped their arms around her. Many tears were shed.

"How did you survive?" Brody asked. "And your eyes. They're…They're glowing!"

"Glowing? Are you sure?" Karma asked.

Brody took out his phone, pulled up a mirror app, and held it up to Karma. She yelped and stared at her reflection in disbelief.

"I…I can't really explain what happened to me. All I remember is the wormhole closed and I was floating. A bright orange light surrounded me. And then…I was engulfed by it. Absorbed. I didn't know where the light ended and I began. I was in and out of consciousness, but when I regained my wits, something had…*shifted* inside of me."

"What do you mean by shifted?" Cole asked.

"I don't know. It's difficult to explain," she answered. She held up her hands and marveled at buzzing electric currents that were crackling across her fingertips. "I could now see thousands of different portals floating around me. They stretched on endlessly in every direction. Somehow I knew that they led to different points in the Master Timeline. There was a tugging sensation in my stomach when I looked at a certain wormhole, and I knew that it would lead me back to all of you."

The twelve Elders slowly approached Cole, Brody, Gabe, and Karma.

"What are you? Don't come any closer!" Karma shouted. Her feet lifted off the ground and she levitated in the air, ready to defend her friends. The three boys stared at her, eyes wide in shock, as ropey electric sparks shot out of her hands.

"It's OK, Karma! These are The Elders. They defeated Thelonia for us!" Brody explained.

"The who?" she asked, slowly sinking back down to the ground.

"The Elders. We are the architects of all reality," a spirit with a bull head said.

"You must know what's happened to Karma then, right?" Cole asked.

"I must admit…I have never seen anything like this before. Let us return to Atmos so that we can convene with Aloicius. We will make sure that all your questions are answered. Does that sound amenable to all of you?"

"I…I guess so," Karma said nervously.

An Elder with a sea goat head moved their hands in a swirling motion and everyone abruptly disappeared.

CHAPTER TWENTY-TWO

Cole's vision slowly cleared and his surroundings came into focus. He, along with Gabe, Brody, and the rest, were standing in the middle of one of the long, mirrored halls of Atmos, but the bubble universe had undergone a drastic transformation. This time it was crowded with robed Uhrzeit members who were moving up and down the hall in dense packs. They were talking excitedly, and their overlapping voices filled the hall with lively chatter.

"Before we speak to Aloicius, I have to see my father. Can you take us to him?" Cole asked.

"Certainly," an Elder with a crab's head said. The humanoid being floated down the hall, Cole and his group following close behind, and the crowds of Uhrzeit gawked and quickly floated out of their way.

When they descended the long stone staircase and came upon the rows of jail cells, a terrible surprise greeted them: Arthur, Sabina, Lucia, and Javier were lying on the floor of their cell. At first, it was hard to tell if they were alive or not. But, upon closer inspection, Cole's stomach unclenched when he saw their chests rising and falling. Their breath was shallow and uneven, and their sickly faces were grey and haggard. Heavy chains bound their wrists and ankles.

"C-Cole? Is that you?" Arthur mumbled weakly.

"Dad!" Cole yelled, and he ran over and stood in front of their jail cell. "What the hell happened to all of you? Please, can someone help me? We need to get them out of there!"

With a wave of their hand, an Elder with a lion head summoned three Uhrzeit members out of thin air and they immediately got to work. The heavy metal doors of the jail cell were quickly pulled off and the prisoners were taken out. Their shackles were removed.

An Uhrzeit member approached Lucia with his hands held up.

"Hey! What are you doing?" Gabe asked nervously.

"All is well. I'm here to help," he said with a reassuring smile. He brought his right hand close to

227

his mouth, put his lips together, and blew. Glittering gold smoke unfurled from his palm and wafted into Arthur, Sabina, Lucia, and Javier's faces. Each of their limbs and torsos suddenly started glowing for several seconds, like a lightbulb that was slowly being illuminated, and when the glow faded, Cole was shocked to see that they all looked healthy again.

"My...My leg!" Arthur cried in astonishment. He jumped to his feet and walked around the room.

"You are all healed," the Uhrzeit member said, bowing slightly. "It's the least we could do after all of the trouble that you've had to endure here."

"We almost starved to death!" Javier yelled. "Not to mention that I saw a man getting *light sucked out of him!* What is going on here?! I demand to speak to whoever is in charge!"

"Of course, sir," the Elder with the set of scales for a head answered. "Let me take you to him now. Aloicius is keen to set things right for everyone."

"Good. Just as long as we don't have to speak to that witch Thelonia," Lucia grumbled.

The Elder made a swiping motion with their hands and the surrounding room abruptly disappeared, only to be immediately replaced with the interior of Saxum Hall. Through his glasses, Cole's eyes fell on a tall, middle-aged man who was seated on a regal throne that was giving off a soft glow. Aloicius, the real version this time, had salt and pepper hair and icy blue eyes. Shimmering silver robes hung off his muscular frame and fell to the floor. His stern face was impassive, yet his eyes burned with a sharp intensity.

"Thank you, Xżsaskélatœntiönüm, as well as the rest of you, for bringing these humans to me. We have much to discuss," he said, nodding his head. The Elder with the set of scales for a head, or Xżsaskélatœntiönüm, nodded in return. At least, that's the name that Cole *thought* he heard, but he had never heard anything like it before, so he couldn't be sure.

"It is good to finally meet you. First of all, I wanted to personally thank Karma, Cole, Gabe, and Brody for everything that you did to save the Master Timeline. You have, quite literally, saved all of reality. Secondly, I wanted to apologize to Lucia, Javier, Arthur, and Sabina. The harsh treatment that you endured while Thelonia controlled Atmos was unacceptable and would never have happened if I had been in charge. Now, I'm sure that you have many questions for me, so please ask anything that you want."

The group was silent for several seconds, unsure of where to begin. Despite his hospitable greeting and the warm welcome that they had received, Aloicius was very intimidating.

"Why can the Uhrzeit talk now?" Brody asked, finally breaking the silence.

"Thelonia removed their ability to speak so that they wouldn't be able to reveal her treachery. A horrible thing to do. When The Elders made her disappear, the Uhrzeit were able to talk again."

"I have a question for The Elders," Cole said, turning to look at them. "I don't mean to be rude, but why do you, um, look the way that you do?"

"Throughout history, we have been called several names, in many different languages; human beings have always felt our presence. You, however, will probably know us as the Zodiac."

Cole felt a wave of recognition roll through him as he looked around at the twelve different Elder beings floating in the room and suddenly recognized Sagittarius, Cancer, Libra, and all of the rest.

"Allow me to interject," said the Elder with a lion head. Everyone's eyes flew to the floating being.

"What is it, Zzwūigeñjkmøntix?" Aloicius asked.

"Something has…shifted. The rules have changed."

"We can all feel it!" said an Elder with the head of a scorpion.

"I have turned my eye inward to look deeply at all that exists, in order to discover the source of this strange feeling that the rest of The Elders have experienced, and what I discovered is unprecedented. Reality has *expanded.* Expanded greatly, in fact. As far I can sense…there is no Master Timeline anymore, thanks to Karma."

"Thanks to me?" Karma asked.

"Organic beings that are exposed to unstable tears in time are ripped apart. However, because you are made of silicone and metal…something unexpected happened. When you entered the tear, the energy that your body produced ricocheted outward and opened pathways to multiple universes."

"M-Multiple universes?" Cole asked softly. His heart started to beat quickly.

"There are now an endless amount of timelines that have been created out of whole cloth. Billions of them, some of them very similar to our own or completely different, are currently branching off our own timeline now. The entire system has changed!"

"So…you're saying that somewhere out there, a version of someone like, say, Bayard Rustin, is living a completely different life?" Brody asked.

"It's very possible," Zzwūigeñjkmøntix replied.

"Is that why I have these, um, *abilities* now?" Karma asked.

"Yes. Temporal energy is pumping through your body as we speak."

Karma's mouth fell open in shock. She held her hands up and they were glowing.

"Hmm…" Aloicius mumbled. He closed his eyes, thinking deeply. In Cole's opinion, this unsmiling and austere man looked just like a large, dour bird who was perched on a nest. "Fascinating. That means that we'll never have to monitor or reset this timeline again. Hmm…I suppose this also means that the Uhrzeit are out of a job. But they are family, so I'll find a use for them. There's still a lot of work to be done."

"I have a question," Javier said. "Can you explain to me what Thelonia was doing when I saw you hooked up to those tubes? I mean…that was crazy."

"It is unfortunate that you had to see that. Thelonia was absorbing my energy, and she used what she was able to acquire to trick some of you into going on her mission and to make that glittering paintbrush. Before you arrived, Thelonia handed me a drink that was laced with poison and I, stupidly, drank it. It paralyzed me immediately and I was in and out of consciousness until now.

Since I cannot be killed, her plan was to drain me of all my energy, until I was nothing more than a dried-up husk, and then she would rule Atmos. She had almost succeeded when The Elders intervened."

"Speaking of Thelonia, back in the Mesozoic Era, she mentioned something called the Time Conflict. She was very vague about it, though. What is it?" Cole asked.

Aloicius's expression darkened. "Ah, yes. The Time Conflict. I'm not surprised that she was vague, seeing how she had a large part in it. Well, it all started during the first Master Timeline. In the year 1324, a human woman named Petronilla changed history. Using a rudimentary wooden time machine, she traveled back in time and killed the lord that had driven over her parents with his chariot. The ensuing damage was so severe that I had no choice but to reset that timeline. Thelonia suddenly went rogue and tried to prevent us from resetting it, injuring twenty Uhrzeit members in the vicious struggle, but they eventually overwhelmed her and placed her in a jail cell, giving me the chance to complete my work. She had always been a bit...different, but I never thought that she was capable of such violence. Anyway, resetting the Timeline was a difficult, but necessary, decision."

"If this woman was so dangerous, then why did you let her out of jail?" Lucia cried.

A prickle of irritation ran down Aloicius's back and he fixed his steely gaze onto her. Lucia's face paled. "Why? Because I wanted to give her a chance to repent. After all, she was imprisoned for twenty centuries. She told everyone that she wanted forgiveness. How was I to know that she was lying?"

"Well…thank you again for saving me and my family. I wish there was some way for me to show you my gratitude," Arthur said.

Aloicius's intense gaze fell onto him. "Actually, Arthur, there is a way. Now that everything has finally been set right, I will be getting rid of *The Astrolabe.* After we send you back to your own time, it will be melted down. Traveling through time is far too dangerous. You must never do it again."

Arthur nodded his head in agreement. "I completely understand. I'm so sorry for all the trouble that I've caused."

"Now, the time has come for all of you to leave Atmos. For your sake, I hope that we don't meet again."

Everyone waved goodbye. Suddenly, a bright flash of light erupted in the air, nearly blinding them, and then they were all transported back to Arthur's laboratory. Everything looked the same as it always did. Soft beams of light poured through a row of windows.

"Look!" Brody cried.

The group stepped back and took in the strange event that was taking place. The large, floating white door with the stained glass at the top, the main entrance to *The Astrolabe,* slowly started to fade away until, after a few moments, it was gone.

"It's…It's all over," Arthur whispered. Bittersweet tears pooled in his eyes and he smiled. "Come on. Let's go find Ruby."

*****

It didn't take long before the group finally reunited with Ruby. In fact, only ten minutes had passed before she suddenly appeared on the manor house doorstep with a beaming smile on her face.

"I knew it! As soon as I saw the sky change back to normal, I just knew that you had fixed the Master Timeline!" she gushed, stepping inside to hug everyone.

"H-Hello Ruby," Karma mumbled sheepishly.

The moment that Ruby caught sight of her, her smile dropped and she stopped in her tracks.

"Oh. Hello."

"Hi."

"You look…different," Ruby said bluntly.

"I have, um, new abilities now. It's a long story."

There was a tense pause.

"Well…anyway," Ruby said, shifting her focus back to the entire group. "You'll all be excited to know that I finally brought down Project Hominum. Once and for all."

"Are you serious?! But how?" Sabina asked in astonishment.

"Well, I got in touch with someone who works for the MCPD, and we teamed up to spring a trap. Most of the members have been taken into custody at this point, but anyone that was missed will be located thanks to a Project Hominum database that Karma and I were given. We don't ever have to worry about them again!"

"My brilliant daughter!" Arthur cried, and he wrapped his arms around her and pulled her in for a hug.

"I can't believe this! They…They've really been punished?" Karma asked in disbelief.

"Yes. Those terrorists will be staying in jail for a long time. Neither Jaxon nor Gustav are included in their numbers, of course, but at least it's something."

Karma nodded, wiping tears from her eyes. "I…I don't know what to say, Ruby. I'm so sorry that I gave up and abandoned you. I should have had more faith in what we were trying to accomplish."

Ruby stared at her intently, an unreadable expression resting on her face. But, after a moment, her mouth curved into a smile and any tension in the room disappeared. "Apology accepted, Karma. You're one of my best friends -- I can't stay mad at you."

They hugged tightly.

"Now, let's find somewhere to catch up!" Ruby said, and everyone cheerfully headed to the kitchen.

The next week flew by in a blurry haze of frenzied activity that was equal parts productive and stressful. The day after they returned to Mechanica City, Arthur received a phone call from President Carver -- she was furious. She raged about the effect that *The Astrolabe* and time travel had had on the country, and it wasn't until he explained that *The Astrolabe* had been permanently decommissioned, even offering to open up his manor house so that her associates could take a look around for proof, that President Carver finally calmed down and stopped scolding him.

The most immediate problem that needed to be faced was Mechanica City itself. There was such an overwhelming amount of destruction, spread throughout the entire city, that they didn't even know where to start. So, they did the only thing that made any sense – they started with their immediate surroundings. Using Ruby's connections with the MCPD, Arthur had officers help Cole, Karma, Gabe, Sabina, and Ruby remove piles of rubble that littered the broken street. They also worked on repairs to the manor house as well as the neighboring houses that had sustained damage.

Cole and Karma strained to lift a heavy concrete pipe that was blocking a neighbor's driveway. It was extremely heavy and kept shifting in their hands. The neighbor and her son looked on.

"I-I can't hold it!" Cole screamed as the pipe slipped from his sweaty hands. It teetered to one side, then the next, and then fell in the direction of the neighbor and her son. But, seconds before they were crushed, Karma threw out her hands and the pipe suddenly froze in midair, giving the woman and her son a chance to scramble out of the way.

"You saved us! H…How did you do that?" the woman asked in disbelief.

Karma stared at her hands, eyes wide in surprise. "I…I don't know! I'm still learning things about myself."

For the rest of the week, she tested out her new abilities. Along with being able to move large objects, as well as levitation, Karma discovered that if she concentrated hard enough, she could project bright energy blasts from her hands that repaired damage. With this newfound knowledge, she decided to fly around the city, repairing holes that had been blown out of the sides of various buildings. The citizens of Mechanica City were so appreciative of her actions to help rebuild the city that any last vestiges of anti-mechanical hate and prejudice disappeared. On a sunny Saturday afternoon, Mayor Simpson awarded her the Medal of Honor during a televised ceremony. Tears of happiness poured down her cheeks as he placed a lanyard with a solid gold medal hanging off it around her neck. Not only that, but she was also made the head of a special task force that would monitor hate crimes against mechanicals and protect them.

Four months later, Cole found himself standing inside a bustling courthouse. The small room, located in City Hall, was packed with people, all of them dressed in their finest attire. Cole was wearing a dark suit with a tie, and as he looked around at his family and friends, a smile crept up his face. A hole in the ceiling that had been haphazardly boarded up allowed a warm breeze to waft into the room.

Cole looked over at his father. Arthur's eyes filled with tears as he watched Sabina, who had just entered the room. Draped in a stunning white wedding gown that fell to the floor, she walked down a carpeted aisle. Cole had never seen her look so radiant and joyful. The dress was covered in small white flowers and bolts of lace.

At the end of the wedding ceremony, the aisle was rolled up so that the reception could begin. The day's events were very low key and humble, but it was full of joy and laughter (not to mention twelve bottles of champagne.)

While Gabe and Cole were dancing on the crowded dance floor with champagne flutes in their hands, Ruby suddenly approached them.

"Hello boys! Having fun?"

Cole wiped sweat off his forehead and stopped dancing. "Absolutely! Hey, who is this?"

Ruby turned and smiled at a handsome blonde man that was standing next to her. "Boys, this is Orlando. He's my...um...can I call you my boyfriend?" She giggled lightly.

"Of course, darling," Orlando replied, blushing deeply. "Gentlemen, it's nice to meet you."

"It's great to meet you!" Cole said. They shook hands.

"Orlando works with the MCPD. He was the one who helped me take down Project Hominum," Ruby said proudly.

Cole's eyes widened in shock. "*Wow*, that's incredible! Thank you for helping her."

"By the way, Ruby, how is your new job?" Gabe asked.

"Oh, it's wonderful! I mean, it's been a big adjustment, and I've had to learn a lot in a short amount of time, but I love being a casting director's assistant. I'm so happy to be back in Mechanica City!"

Time marched on. Soon it was the middle of June, and graduation had finally arrived. Four years of hard work had led to this moment, and there was so much nervous anticipation leading up to the ceremony that Cole sometimes felt like his head was spinning. On the big day, he was sitting with the rest of his classmates in an echoing event hall inside the Mechanica City Center. When Professor Khan called his name, he rose to his feet, wearing a black graduation cap and gown, and made his way to the stage where his favorite teacher was handing out diplomas. Photographer drones floated in front of the stage and snapped pictures, their flashbulbs popping on and off.

When he finally walked across the stage and received his diploma, he took a moment to bask in the applause and good feelings that were beaming at him from the audience; his friends and family were jumping up and down and cheering for him. Professor Khan shook his hand and pinned a pair of tiny silver wings onto his graduation cap. He hugged her and smiled, feeling like fireworks were popping in his chest.

A halcyon summer awaited the boys. Mechanica City was slowly coming back to life, and Brody, Cole, and Gabe spent every day together, soaking in their last free summer before adult responsibilities came calling. When Gabe wasn't at work and when Brody wasn't at his internship, the boys went to museums, drank in bars, and danced in nightclubs until the sun came up. It was the best summer of Cole's life.

On the first of August, the moment had finally arrived -- Brody was moving to New York City. However, he was no longer going there *just* to start his acting career. After being inspired by all of the wondrous things that he saw during his adventures on *The Astrolabe,* he decided to enroll in the Master's in History program at NYU. Brody had always thought that he could only be one thing, but recent events had caused him to rethink everything. The world is a large place and he wanted to grab every experience that he could grasp.

Cole and Gabe accompanied Brody to Aronaxx Station in order to see him off. The train station was packed that morning, and men and women wearing traveling clothes hurried past them. Cole felt a lump of sadness in his throat, but, with considerable effort, he managed to ignore it.

A train whistle sounded. Brody turned to Cole and Gabe, suitcases in hand, and said, "Well…that's me! Time to go."

"As soon as you get settled, call us up and we'll come for a visit," Cole said.

"Absolutely! We'll have so much fun together." Brody paused, his eyes filling with tears. "Thank you for everything. I'll never forget what we went through together."

The three boys hugged, and then Brody boarded the train. As the locomotive left the station, he turned around and waved at Cole and Gabe through the window. Then, turning back around, he smiled and settled into his seat, ready to start his new life.

After a week-long search, Cole and Gabe finally found their dream home. They chose a two-bedroom apartment on the seventh floor of a sleek gold skyscraper that stood on a tree-lined street. The neighborhood was ideal due to its proximity to Nautique, and it was bordered on two sides by other apartment buildings as well as lush parks. Even though it was in the heart of downtown Mechanica City, the area was quiet and tucked away from the hustle and bustle.

One afternoon, Cole was standing inside his living room hanging up a framed piece of paper. After a few adjustments, he smiled and took a step back to admire his work. The framed piece of paper was hanging next to several framed photos that covered the wall: Gabe standing next to his grandmother Camila; a group shot of Brody, Cole, and Gabe; Ruby and Orlando at the beach on vacation; an old photo of Cole smiling with his mom. He smiled and breathed a contented sigh -- he hadn't had a panic attack in months.

Suddenly, there was the sound of a doorknob turning and the front door opened.

"You're back!" Cole said. Gabe let himself inside and shut the door.

"Hey babe! What are you up to?"

"Oh, just hanging up my job acceptance letter," Cole said with pride. "I officially signed a contract with the Mechanica Aviation Bureau a couple of hours ago!"

"You did? Congratulations! You're so impressive to me."

Cole blushed. "Thanks. The Mechanica Aviation Bureau is a great company. During the interview process, I immediately felt confident and comfortable speaking with them. Very different from my Technicus Incorporated interview. I guess that saving the entire universe a few times has a way of making other things seem not as intimidating. I felt confident and sure of myself! My first day is in a week. I'm actually pretty excited!"

"You should be excited!" Gabe said. "After everything that you've been through, I know that you'll do a fantastic job at the Mechanica Aviation Bureau."

"It's going to be a great new start!"

"Come here," Gabe said with a smile, and Cole walked over and hugged him. The two boys moved to the window, arms around each other, and watched the setting sun.

ABOUT THE AUTHOR

Kyle Cornell currently lives in Richmond, Virginia with his husband and two Pomeranians. When not working for arts organizations in the city, Kyle enjoys reading insane Internet articles and watching reality TV shows about drag queens. Visit www.mechanicacity.com.

Made in the USA
Columbia, SC
26 August 2024

41179115R00135